Crack Spell

Crack Spell

Keith Norton

iUniverse, Inc.
Bloomington

Crack Spell

iUniverse books may be ordered through booksellers or by contacting:

iUniverse
1663 Liberty Drive
Bloomington, IN 47403
www.iuniverse.com
1-800-Authors (1-800-288-4677)

ISBN: 978-1-4502-6270-5 (sc)
ISBN: 978-1-4502-6271-2 (ebk)

Printed in the United States of America

iUniverse rev. date: 12/18/2010

This book is dedicated to my mother Angela 'Fuzz' Noisette...From September 12, 1946 to Eternity, I love you Ma with everything I've got...Your son Keith

You know many people indulge in the usage of crack cocaine, in just the activity of smoking it, alone it could be a hobby; something to do. The process of putting a gun or stem together.

Hearing the sizzling sound that the crack makes when the flame hits that ladrello or brick of cooked cocaine. It sounds like putting a seasoned thick rib-eye steak into a scorching hot pan. Seeing the smoke that's in the glass is exciting to some. Yes, while the coke smoke is taking effect in the pleasure space of your brain…stimulating you to the highest degree; what goes up must come down and the fall or come down of the crack high is as devastating as they come. Some just love the taste of cocaine-smoke.

Yes indeed, there are a lot of reasons why people smoke crack-cocaine. But I've never to see anyone master that high, to where they won't steal, sell or pawn there valued possessions. I've never seen a crack smoker smoke crack and sit and have a sociable dinner with people. It Kills, Steals and Rob you for your very life. The crack abuser must put an end to crack abusing or crack abusing will put an end to the crack abuser.

Crack Spell

Judy, Nancy and Teresa, Teeka for short, were sitting around Judy's living room, drinking and talking along with a little music to illuminate the atmosphere. All three of the ladies are very attractive, and with all of the physical and mental beauty these ladies posses will be quickly and surely taken away from them by the maliciously deadly crack-rock.

The three ladies were sitting on the sofa around Judy's coffee table, when Nancy pulls out a bent malt-liquor can, and a folded piece of aluminum foil full of cigarette ashes, along with a lighter and a slab of crack-cocaine. Nancy put the brick on the table and proceeded to slice it up into small pieces with a razor blade. She then took one of the pieces and placed it on the ashes that sat atop the poked holes in the short malt-liquor can. Nancy took a lighter that was lying on the table and flicked it and placed the flame on the crack that was sitting on top of the ashes. She inhaled and pulled her mouth away from the can.

"Tension, damn that shit is Tension," Nancy said as a little drop of spittle appeared through her thick beautiful lips.

As she leaned back on the sofa she mounted up a bigger piece and inhaled. Her thick thighs came apart as she exhaled the smoke slowly out of her nose. Judy and Teresa were looking in curious admiration; both saw bliss on Nancy's face. Teresa quickly grabbed the can to imitate Nancy's actions, Nancy quickly tapped Teresa on her knee and motioned to both of them silently, moving slowly as she put another set of ashes on top of the ones that were already on the can.. Nancy then put

1

a big piece of crack on the ashes and handed the can to Teresa. Teresa took a blast of the dope; her eyes squinted as she put the can down on the coffee table quietly and slowly. Teresa then started gazing at Nancy between her legs; she then proceeded to lift up the short grey skirt that Nancy wore and peeled her light green satin panties to the side and started licking and sucking Nancy's pussy.

"Umm, yeah taste it like that," were Nancy's comments. Intrigued and amused by the other two ladies actions, Judy couldn't wait to inhale the drug. She mounted a huge piece of the dope and inhale while Teresa and Nancy were admiring each other sexually. Judy put the lighter's flame to the crack and inhaled slowly; she held in the smoke and exhaled slowly. Judy's mouth twisted and her teeth clamped tight together. Teresa and Nancy stopped and watched as Judy was being captivated by the intensity of the crack smoke. Judy put the can down, and slowly walked over to the two women and got undressed. She slowly sat next to Teresa, cupped her breast and squeezed. They started getting into some heavy sexual activity.

While Teresa and Judy were in a sexual frenzy, Nancy mounted up another piece, she hit it and watched Judy and Teresa get into a 69 as she lay back on the couch smoking a Newport cigarette. The same continued for an half an hour, until the ladies were realizing that they were out of crack to smoke. As they all sat around wondering about more crack and how to get it- Judy asked Nancy if she could get more,

"Yea, all I'll have to do is call her, let me see that phone, let me see her number is." Nancy started dialing,

"Hello," Nancy said. Tonya, the dealer picked up the phone.

"What's up?" Tonya asked.

"What's up girl, this Nancy."

"Yeah, how was that." Tonya was referring to the crack she sold her earlier.

"Oh damn, that shit was fire, you got anymore of that… that there was some grade".

"Yeah, about how much do you need?" Tonya asked.

"Hold on let me ask my girl. Judy how much you got?" Nancy asked quickly.

"Is one-fifty alright?" Judy asked.
"Hell yeah." Nancy answered emphatically.
"One-fifty, how long will you be?"
"Bout twenty."
"I'm here at that house you dropped me off to earlier."
"On Gum Street?" Tonya asked.
"Yeah"You there… alright I'm on my way."
"Cool." Nancy said.
"Alright, One." Tonya said and closed her cell phone.

Tonya is 5-6 … 172 lbs, small waist, thick thighs and ass, smooth skin and gorgeous face. Twenty minutes later Tonya pulled up in metallic black Cadillac Escalade, and blew the horn. All three of the women were now fully dressed. Nancy peeped through the blinds to see if it was Tonya,
"Yeah, that's her, give me the money."
Judy gave her the money and Nancy went outside to cop the dope. Nancy got inside of the Cadillac and closed the door.

"What's up?" Nancy asked.

Tonya opened up her hand and gave Nancy two huge cookies of freshly cooked crack slabs each worth 100 dollars apicce. Nancy looked and asked about the relationship Tonya is in with a guy named Tim. Tonya's son Mack's dad.
"Everything is alright but I need to get rid of that quick, the motherfuckah is silly as hell, that it vexes my fucking spirit to even talk about it." This nigga is not even up with the times, all the bullshit arguing and saying dumb slick shit out of his mouth. Everything seems to be backwards with this motherfucker. I do what I need to do for my kids benefit. Even though I hustle I'm in church service every Sunday. I've got faith that I'll be delivered from all this hustling dope shit, but that nigga's out of my life as far as I'm concerned. I'm splitting the rent with this motherfucker so it's convenient, but not even that shit won't last because he lost his job, and as far as touching and fucking a silly motherfucker, that's out of the question."
Nancy looked at Tonya with a smooth gaze.
"So what are you going to do?" Nancy asked.

"I'm through with that, but girl give me a call and you know I don't fuck around with this shit at night, that's my kid's time, doing homework and shit-- teaching. Nancy didn't say a word; instead she hopped out of the truck and thanked Tonya for the deal. Tonya drove off. Nancy entered the house; both Teresa and Judy were sitting there in anticipation. Nancy put the blocks of crack on the table.

Pi-Dow! Nancy exclaimed.

Teresa's face could've been sitting on some type of amusement park billboard, Judy's face also, even though she didn't understand what was going on fully, all she knew was that they all had enough crack to smoke for a while.

"Girl give me some of that shit now, I got to have it." Judy stated.
"Chill girl, this time we're going to feel the full effect." Nancy remarked.
"Can I get that antenna?"
"What antenna?" Judy asked.
"The one on the back of the T.V., can I get it girl? I'm telling you we're going to feel the full effect, we're going to smoke lovely this time, watch this." Nancy stated convincingly.

Nancy walked over to the T.V. and broke off one of the antennas, came back to her seat on the couch and broke the large end of the antenna, about 4 inches of it, then she grabbed her purse and pulled out some new Char-boy. She took the scissors that were on the coffee table and cut a piece of the brillo pad, just enough to fit to the tip of the antenna stem. Nancy then burned the small piece of Char- Boy with the lighter, to burn off all of the chemicals.

Nancy then put the small piece of burned Char-Boy in the tip of the stem and packed it in using the tip of a metal clothing hanger. She broke a piece of the crack and melted it on top of the stem, she gestured for Judy to come sit next to her. She put the pulling end to Judy's mouth then lit it. Nancy instructed her to pull slow and steady as she was pulling Nancy told her to pull and give the stem some air, as Judy did this Nancy lowered the stem parallel with the room, as a cloud of smoke filled her mouth. Judy quickly jerked away from the stem. A thick cloud of smoke traced the outside of Judy's face.

"There it is," Nancy said smiling, "Y'all see what I'm talking bout." Judy frowned and squinted then laid back on the couch with pleasure.

"You felt that?" Teresa asked Judy, but she couldn't respond because the dope was so potent and butter. Nancy then mounted another slug of the crack and put it on the stem and handed it to Teresa. Teresa took her a blast, as Judy slowly got up, grabbed the stereo's remote and pressed play. Out poured the sounds of 'Reunion' off of Maxwell's CD, 'Urban Suit'.

"Damn, that's my shit, I like that shit right there," excitedly exclaimed Nancy.

Nancy broke two more pieces of the antenna and made crack stems, now each of the ladies had their own gun (stem). Tonya pulled up in the driveway of her house. Tim the dad of her youngest child was under the car porch smoking Dirties (cocaine laced with weed in a blunt) with a partner of his. Tonya got out of the Escalade and verbally fired off on Tim.

"My man, what's up with you smoking that shit round my house my nigga," Tonya said.
"Man, gone ahead with that shit…you're always buggin." Tim said, while his partner sat quietly while smoking the laced El.
"I really need for you to vamp my nigga," Tonya said.
"Well if I have to leave then I'm telling the Babylon (police) that you up in here serving all this hard."
Tonya looked shocked and surprised, then said…
"Fuck you nigga!", and rushed into the house with two plastic bags of groceries in her hand.

Tonya has two kids; the dad of eldest of her children is doing Life in the state Penitentiary for being a habitual Felon and caught with a loaded firearm. Tonya is a very clean and bright young lady. She was raised in one of the roughest areas of town, and because she was so attractive in high school all of the guys were blood hounding her.
Tonya was well developed and it caught the attention of the neighborhood drug dealer, who quit school after the ninth grade. The

young man was twenty and saw Tonya walking home from school when he struck up a conversation. They started dating then she became pregnant. Tonya delivered her first child in the eleventh grade. And due to her exceptional basketball ability she earned Parade All-American honors as a senior and received a full scholarship to attend De Paul University. Her mother looked after her daughter while she attended college. She majored in Education and Psychology. Her GPA was a 3.0 until she got pregnant again, this time after her junior year in college. She was forced to drop out and face her responsibilities. Tonya dropped out of college and went back home to live with her mother.

Tonya was at home now living with her mother and her daughter Tracy, who's eight, while pregnant with Tim's son. She met Tim at a barbeque she was invited to. Tim at the time was working as a Cherry Picker at a grocery store warehouse and selling a little powder on the side. After the barbeque Tim drove her to her mother's house. They dated heavy and Tonya was really into Tim mainly because he helped her with her daughter Tracy. Every weekend Tim would take them both to the zoo or the movies or they'd go to the mall and just walk the strip.

Tonya had no job and no vehicle. Tim told her that she could make a little money on the side by serving crack-cocaine. One evening on his way home from work he stopped by the dope hole and brought ten juggling dimes for Tonya, when they went out that night he told her that she could sell'em, just give a taste to a smoker in her mom's neighborhood and the customers would automatically come.

She did that to the tune of five-hundred dollars a day, just sitting out in her mother's front yard. Two years had past and Mack her second child was born, Tim's son, and she had upped her crack selling occupation to a full time livelihood or hustle.

She purchased a Cadillac Escalade from a onetime owner. They had moved in together. Tim's obsession for marijuana had become a bit of a problem. The place where he was employed gave him a random drug test, and he failed. They fired him and that's when the tension between Tim and Tonya started. He started getting down and not looking for another place to work. Tonya would have been okay with him, if he would have shown some type of effort to get back on his feet. And all Tim seemed to do was smoke marijuana and lay around the house. So a bit of resentment was built up in Tonya to look at Tim as being weak. She looks at it as if to say…

"With this nigga I won't make it, because if he runs into an obstacle in the future, he gets depress like a bitch, and won't continue to look for an opportunity until he's successful…I don't want a bitch, I want a man." She often mused.

She was tired of the entire situation and wanted a new start and better environment for her children, so she pack up her and the kid's things in the SUV, about 4 in the morning, and headed up the 95 North highway until she arrived in Atlanta. There, she sheltered it a bit until she found adequate housing which was fast because she has kids. From there she utilized her credits she received from DePaul, which were six credits away from a Bachelors and landed a Vice Principals position in the Atlanta school's district. And because she was so self-reliant; she purchases a home in the suburbs of the city.

The ladies were perplexed and Judy was wondering if they could get more crack for her to smoke.

"Do you think you can get some more of that," Judy asked Nancy sort of pitifully desperate, as Teresa gathered herself and sat back on the sofa.

"Here girl, drink some of this straight gin to get that edge off of you," Nancy suggested. Nancy had been sipping on the straight liquor all the while, that's why she was the calmest of the three. There were two extra glasses on the coffee table. So Nancy poured each of the ladies a glass out of the Fifth of Seagram's Gin she had sitting at the end of the couch. And after Judy and Teresa both took heavy gulps of the gin, they both mellowed afterwards, but they all still wanted to smoke more crack.

"Damn girl that shit is good, but it keeps you wanting it. Damn, they call this a cheap form of cocaine…I doubt it. All I want now is some more of that shit. Do you think you can call ya girl again?" Judy asked desperately.

"She doesn't serve at night," Nancy said, She continued. "But I know those lil dudes down on the corner in that grey and white house… now they got some Fire ass dope!" Nancy exclaimed.

"Judy, you got some more money?" Nancy asked Judy.

"Yeah I got some money, but it's the two-hundred sixty dollars I had for my light bill, it's due tomorrow night."

"You get this for us girl, and I'll pay you back tomorrow!" Teresa exclaimed.

"How are you going to pay me back?" Judy asked.

"Spend a hundred dollars and I'll give it back to you tomorrow, for real girl!" Teresa kept pleading in hopes to get another blast off of the pipe.

"I'll help her pay it back," Nancy remarked (That was the dope talking).

Judy was looking out of the window, paranoid thinking that someone was casing where they were, and what they were doing. She was ghosting.

"How long will you be?" Judy asked.

"A couple of minutes," answered Nancy.

"Give me your jacket girl, it's getting chilly outside." Nancy stated.

"Go ahead, just hurry back," said Judy.

Nancy stepped out on Judy's porch and closed the door behind her. She proceeded to walk down to where Skip and his three associates were slinging and hustling crack. All of them were smoking Blunts of 'Black Jamaican Ganja,' and listening to the track of OC's 'Sronjay,' off of the Jewels CD. Nancy gets there and knocks on the door; one of Skip's associates comes to the door and asked who is it.

"Skip this is Nancy, one of the ladies at Faye's crab boil today." Nancy quickly answered.

Even though she smokes crack, Nancy has the beauty and figure of a very manageable young lady. Earlier that day Nancy was looking rather sexy to Skip and the fellas. And Skip has had it on his mind to meet her. Nancy had never met Skip before, but she knew he sold dope. Sometimes Faye smokes, but when she does, she only smokes 'Juice'(crack crushed up in tobacco or marijuana). Faye has never smoked crack raw, she has always lased it with something. In one of Faye's earlier sessions Nancy was there and she let Nancy try the crack she was lacing- Nancy of course had a straight shooter (crack stem) with her and tested some of Skip's dope raw. That's how she knew he sold crack. Skip got up and came to the door.

"Yeah, you're that pretty sister who had on that black skirt today, right?" Skip asked.

"Yeah, that was me," Nancy replied.

"What's up?" Skip asked.

"I need a hundred dollars worth of that good hard." Nancy stated.

"Hold on," he said.

Skip closed the door and went to the back of the house to the safe, where he had a pet python, a ton of cash and some of the purest cooked coke in the area. He cut her up about a hundred and forty dollars worth of thick chunked blocks and put them in a zip lock sandwich bag. He closed the safe and headed for the front of the house, with the dope in hand he calmly stepped over his fellas who were then listening to 'It is what it is,' by Cassidy. Skip opened the door and handed Nancy the baggy full of cooked rock.

"Here ya go, baby girl." She gave Skip the money; he counted it, as Nancy headed down the three flights of stairs.

"Hey! Come back and see me alright!"

"Alright." Nancy quickly answered.

In a hurry to get to Judy's house, she began to walk quickly. Nancy arrived at the house, walked through the gate and closed it. She didn't have to knock on the door; Teresa and Judy were standing there with the door open even though the temperature was steadily dropping. Nancy step into the door, the baggy of crack was stuffed in her panties. Nancy walked past the two ladies saying,

"Damn it's getting cold out there. I got to go to the restroom," even though the ladies looked surprised and wanted a bump of dope, they said nothing. Nancy got to the restroom and closed the door then removed the sack of dope from her panties and sat down to take a piss…

"Damn that feels good," Nancy said of releasing the urine from her body, after she wiped herself clean with a wet tissue.

She pulled up her panties from around her calves and sat on the edge of the bathtub. She grabbed the baggy of dope from the floor and placed it on the edge of the bathtub, reached inside of the baggy and broke a nice piece of the block of crack she had just purchased, and hid it. She hid the piece of dope in an empty opaque medicine bottle that was in the medicine cabinet. She then hid the bottle in the cabinet behind some gauze and cough medicine, after that Nancy headed for the living room where the ladies were patiently waiting. Nancy placed the baggy of crack on the living room table, sat down and emptied the crack on the table. Even though Nancy had cuffed some of the crack, it still looked to be a 'God Father Deal,' (more crack for the money they spent).

Nancy then cut up all of the fresh dope into chunks, melted her a nice piece on top of the stem she had. She didn't pull on it, but sat back cool, looking at Judy and Teresa mount themselves up a piece on top of their stems. Nancy flicks the lighter and teases the stem with the flame as she was puffing, as an old man would do when he lights a tobacco pipe. The base was what was happening and nothing else when Nancy released the smoke coolly out of her nose, her pussy immediately juiced up. She couldn't speak; the dope was 'Straight Butter'. It's late and the living room is dim lit with candles burning. Its 12 midnight as you can hear the smooth crackle sound when fire hits cooked cocaine.

All three of the ladies slowly hold the smoke in and smoothly exhale repeatedly.

Nancy mounts up again and takes a power blast and as she is hitting the dope, she slowly grabs Teresa's head and guides Teresa's mouth towards her pussy. Teresa sucks Nancy's pussy with reckless abandon while Judy walks to the end of the couch where Nancy's head is, then sits on the sofa's arm. Judy slowly hits another piece, and while she's exhaling the smoke slowly out of her nose she slowly bends to spread open her ass cheeks with both hands as she backs into Nancy's mouth, then slowly placed the stem and lighter quietly on the floor. Judy had her ass cheeks spread, while Nancy put her hands on Judy's cheeks to stretch them even wider and proceeded to lick. Nancy sucked hard at Judy's heaven, as Teresa fingered Nancy's quim.

The dope was drop. The crack was the finest Nancy has ever smoked. The dope was strong and it tasted good. The lady's went on sexing and smoking, switching positions and incorporating sex toys into the party.

All the while Lisa, Judy's sister had Judy's two daughters along with her daughter with her. They were enjoying their day watching DVD's over at Lisa's, suddenly Lisa gets a call on her cell phone.

"Hello," voiced Lisa, when she answered her phone.
"Yeah, this T, the guy you met at the Nation's Foods last night."

Tim was outside waxing his vehicle. While Tonya, was inside finishing cooking Sunday's dinner, which is a ritual for Tonya and her mother, her sister and two of her aunts which are close in age with Tonya. Tonya's at her kitchen stove discussing how she wants Tim out of her life. Then one of her aunts replies…

"Tonya, just don't throw any pot-ash and hot syrup on him, or do anything silly that would land you behind bars."

"Yeah, there are more ways than one, that will make him leave you," commented her sister, she continued on, "You can always cut the loving off. Just don't fuck with him, that's how you do that, just straight stop fucking with him. At all cost, keep yourself out of those people system…jail is straight up hell." She continued, "Or if it comes down to it …shit, you can pack up and leave that motherfuckah!"

Tonya's relatives do not know of her activities of selling rock.

They figured that the little three day a week professional job she has and Tim's income was maintaining her and her girls. But they really didn't care about the insignificant. All they cared about was Tonya's efficacy, regardless if she had or didn't have. Meanwhile, outside, Tim was setting things up with Lisa, waxing his car listening to 'Pussy Ass Nigger'by Luke Skywalker and the 2 live crew, off of the album 'Move Something'.

"So I'm coming over right, and we're going to get into something." Tim stated.

"We can, I'm spending the day with my daughter and Two nieces, but when this day is done, they're hitting the bed and I guess you can come over, do you know where I'm at?" Lisa asked.

"Nah, where?" Tim asked.

"I'm over here on Brideir, 555 Brideir Street on the North side."

"Alright I'll be there tonight." Tim quickly replied

"Well, when I put them to bed about nine, which should be a good time.

"That's straight," Tim said.

"Alright bye," Lisa closed her cell and Tim continued to wash his car.

M eanwhile, Tonya, her mother, sister, aunts and her children are sitting
around the table eating Sunday dinner. And at Judy's house, the
girls were still smoking, but they were again at their last end of crack
to smoke.

"We need some more," Teresa stated. "Nancy you got any more
loot?"

Nancy shook her head, no.

Teresa started ghosting on the floor, picking the carpet in hopes to
find a piece of a crumb to smoke. All she seemed to come up with was
lint. Nancy said that she needed to go to the restroom; Teresa and Judy
paid her no mind, and continued to smoke up the remaining crumbs
of crack that was left on the coffee table, and looking for more on the
carpet. Nancy steps in the restroom and quickly gets the medicine
bottle out of the medicine cabinet filled with the crack that she had
hidden earlier.

Nancy quietly sat on the edge of the bathtub and started smoking
heavily. She was smoking so hard that she forgot the time she was in
there. Judy and Teresa were pitifully geeking and desperate for another
hit of dope. Then they started wondering what was taking Nancy so long
to return from the restroom. They both decided to kill their curiosity by
going to check on Nancy. Teresa and Judy passed the kitchen as Judy
begins to hear a loud crackling sound coming from her bathroom. Judy
kicked open the door and attacks Nancy.

"Dirty Hoe, we're out here on the floor looking for a crumb to smoke and you're in here smoking... bitch I'll kill you!"

Judy's rage had gone overboard and Nancy was trying to get out of Judy's grasp. Teresa played the wall in the hallway, as Judy picked up a porcelain object and strikes Nancy in the forehead with it. Blood begin to leak heavily from Nancy's forehead, as she saw an opening and ran out of the house. Teresa looked at Judy in frightened shock, as Judy told Teresa,

"Get out of my house right now Hoe, or I'll kill you."

Teresa ran with recklessness out of Judy's house, as Judy quickly closed the door, looked at the mess in the living room and fell to the floor in tears. She cried and cried, then slowly realized that her sister Lisa was bringing her children home, so she slowly picked up the place. Judy went to hit her light switch and the lights wouldn't come on. Her electricity was turned off. She then thought that she had to get herself together before her kids got home.

She hurried and took a quick shower, lit a few scented candles, put on something comfortable and waited for her children. Thirty minutes had passed and there was a knock on the door. She peeked through the blinds to see who it was; it was Lisa and the kids.

Judy opened the door and quickly stepped out to avoid Lisa from noticing that her lights were off.
"Hey, y'all had a good time?" as she quickly lets her two daughters into the house and closed the door behind them. She hugged her sister Lisa and told her thank you and hugged her niece. Lisa looked into her sister's eyes and could tell something was wrong. Lisa then asked Judy if she was alright.

"Yeah, I guess I'll be okay," responded Judy.
"Nah, for real girl, what's wrong? Lisa asked her sister again.
Judy just shook her head no, rather reserved like.
"Well, if you need anything," Lisa told her, "Let me know."
"Nah, I just need some rest," Judy said.

"Well, we're going to be leaving now, Call my cell alright."
"Alright, I love y'all."

"We love you too," Lisa said, as she walked carefully down the stairs with her daughter. They got into her vehicle and drove off. Judy was confused about the entire situation. The pleasure of smoking crack left her dumbfounded and broke, there was no money to get her electricity back on, and no funds to buy groceries, it was all up in the air in crack smoke.

She felt bad inwardly, her insides literally felt parched. She suddenly thought about her two daughters. The crack episode had only brought trouble to her. She needed money to cut her lights back on. So she decided to call her Aunt Donna and uncle Juice for the money. Her uncle Juice and Aunt Donna have been married for thirty plus years.

Uncle Juice is a retired editor and publisher of Black Literary works and Aunt Donna is and has been for a third of their marriage a very prominent and respected Image Consultant. She mainly works with young ladies that are from the ages 13 to 21 years old. She teaches them how to respect their bodies and get a full education in the schools and at home. She teaches the young women to choose education over early pregnancy. Not to fall victim to drugs and to respect and love their parents at anytime.

She takes the young women who are at the crossroad and brings them to church in her van. Scripture reading during the week is mandatory. For the young women who don't have at least two dresses, she gets them clothing from a clothing drive that Juice has once a month. The clothing is quality and none of the young women feels subordinate or inferior when they attend church. Donna's observation was: if they look okay, and have a full stomach, they'll be able to grasp Christ's teachings better.

Uncle Juice is well remembered internationally for his trailblazing campaign in removing white pictorial biblical images in black households. His complaint was: A white Jesus sitting with twelve white men, at the 'The Last Supper'. He challenged every single black household nationally to remove such damaging material from around their children.

His point was this, why should black parents work to pay bills and raise their children orderly and come to have Sunday dinner around a portrait of the Son of God and the twelve Disciples portrayed as being white or Caucasian. The campaign was a success internationally. Uncle Juice now travels around the U.S fulfilling speaking engagements at different learning institutions around the country.

Judy dials the number and the answering machine comes on. 'APOLOGIZE, WE'RE OUT OF THE COUNTRY...WE'LL BE BACK IN A WEEK. PLEASE LEAVE A MESSAGE.' Judy seemed puzzled; she sat on the edge of the sofa and wept quietly.

She told her girls that there was a problem with the lights and it will be fixed quickly. She gathered herself together, went to the refrigerator and fixed them each a glass of juice and gave them fruit- before telling them to get their clothing ready for the next day of school. She then lit an extra scented candle for their room.

All the while at Lisa's house, Lisa was getting ready for her date with Tim. Her daughter was in the bed sleep, getting rest for the next school day. Lisa, took a warm quick shower, then put on some sexy lingerie apparel. Her thick ass cheeks and hips protruded out of the black thong she wore and her thick thighs were overlaying the expensive stocking tops. She also wore a black robe that was full-length and satin. She put on a mixed CD of sultry hits old and new, that she purchased from the local flea market.

There was a knock at the door, and then a door bell ring. Lisa sensuously asked who was it- Tim responded that it was him. She peeped through the peep hole of the door and let him in. Tim was speechless and mumbled not a word. He was completely hypnotized by Lisa's beauty and style. She then gestured for to him to have a seat as she walked to the other side of the sofa... picking up the remote to lower the music. She asked if he wanted a glass of cognac... "Yes," Tim answered.

"So what do you do?" Lisa asked.
"I own my company."
"That's nice, replied Lisa.

As she sat the Liquor down on the coffee table, she took a seat and slightly parted her legs. Giving Tim a full view of her pussy that was visible as the thong was snugged inside of her Mound of Venus. Tim slowly lowered his face to her smooth midsection.

Lisa then grabbed the back of his head with her left hand and guided Tim's face towards her love as she spread her thighs as far as she could.

Tim lowered himself to his knees and proceeded to suck Lisa out. The scent of Lisa was fresh and feminine. Lisa undid her bra; she started to moan loudly as she begins to release the sexual tension she'd been logging around for weeks. They soon took the heated sexual episode to the bedroom. They explored every kind of position, and when Tim switched on the lamp he couldn't believe how appetizing she was when he saw her laying on her stomach and one of her stockings was down at her calf.

Later that morning she quickly told Tim that they couldn't be an item, and he would have to leave because she had to get her daughter off to school. No breakfast, no time to watch the morning news, nothing. It was disheartening for Tim, but some pills you have to swallow. He wanted more with Lisa, but she didn't want more with him.

All the while, Nancy had to receive forty-one stitches near her left temple. She was released from the hospital and headed for Faye's house. Faye was on her front lawn bar-b-cuing and frying fish. Faye asked Nancy if she was o.k. Nancy responded, yes.

"But I need a place to stay," humbly retorted Nancy.

"Nancy I've got three bedrooms in there, and you know we're down. I also have some clothes that will fit you... you straight, I got you, alright"

"Faye, thank you." Nancy said.

"You can go in there and take a shower, and look in that bottom-right drawer, it's about five or six different outfits in there that you can wear and this food should be ready soon." Faye stated.

The warmth of Faye's friendship lifted Nancy's spirits, and she no longer felt down about the altercation she had with Judy.

"Thank you again," Nancy said as a tear streamed down her cheek.

"Don't even try it, just go in there and get straight, you know how we do." Faye stated.

They embrace, then Nancy went inside of the house. She retrieves an out-fit and takes a long warm shower. She steps out of the shower and heads for the room to dry off, and put on the fresh clothing she retrieved from Faye's dresser drawer. While she is dressing she spots the Holy Bible on Faye's dresser, she stops what she is doing and decides to read a scripture out of it. The verses she read was out of the book of John, 8th chapter: verses 3through 21. And after she read that she became more focus on what she should do about her current addiction to crack cocaine. And as we all know, that brief moment of righteousness soon changes to corruption, fast. She then put the bible back onto the dresser, took one of Faye's pain pills, put a new gauze bandage over the stitches and headed outside. Faye noticed the bandage and wanted to know exactly what had happened.

"For real, what happened down there with ya'll?"

"I prefer not to even talk about it"; Nancy continued, "Anyway what's happening with you and ya boy across the street?" Nancy asked, she was referring to Skip the neighborhood crack dealer.

"Talking about Skip, yeah he's over there," Faye said. She continued, "He went somewhere, but before he left I copped this fat dub of powder from him."

Faye had the powder sitting on a compact mirror along with a razor blade. She chopped the coke up on the mirror, and then she rolled up a dollar very tightly and took a big toot.

"Damn, that nigga always have the fly ass shit, you want some?" She asked Nancy.

Faye passes the coke to Nancy. Nancy took a one on one, and then passes the compact of coke back to Faye. Skip then pulls up, he gestures for Nancy to come over to him. Nancy tells Faye to excuse her and walks across the street.

"How about handling some things at this place while I'm away," Skip stated to her.

"What sort of things"? Nancy asked.

"You know cleaning and laundry, things like that, plus I got some ideas for you to make some good money… you with that?"

"It depends on how much you are paying."

"About seventy dollars a day and you won't have to worry about any bills or dope to smoke. You know what? You're fine as hell, why don't you step inside of the house so we could discuss this in more detail."

Nancy followed Skip inside. The place was fashionably decorated complete with a sixty-four inch flat screen, a five piece sectional and a full bar, and as he was escorting her to view the rest of the house, Nancy couldn't help but see the 70's style bowl pipe that sat hellishly on the coffee table. After they had checked out the entire house, Skip led her back to the living room and told her to have a seat. Nancy sat next to Skip as he pulled out a five hundred dollar bomb. Fifty thick pieces of crack was in a plastic baggy.

Trevor 'Skip' Karp took one of the pieces out and place it on the bowl pipe, handed Nancy a lighter then sat back. Nancy hit the thick piece of crack that was on the bowl. The taste and tension of the dope was grade A. Skip knew he had her then. As she was putting the pipe down, Skip got up and headed for the door, and on his way out of the door he dropped four more of the pieces on the floor and told her to clean up, then he left.

Nancy sat up and tried to get herself together. She went over and got the pieces off of the floor and went to sit back on the sofa. She chopped one of the pieces with her thumbnail, placed it on the bowl and lit it, as she pulled slowly she laid back and spread her thighs and placed her right hand in her panties. She sat the pipe down and euphoria from the tension of the dope was ecstasy. A dribble of slob escape the left corner of her mouth, she quickly wiped it away and messaged her vagina.

After she had satisfied herself with an explosive orgasm and another hit of the pipe, she walked over to the bar and poured herself a large shot of Hennessey. The Hennessey took that geek and desperate craving off of her. As she felt herself calming down she decided to smoke a Newport cigarette and take another walk through the house. As she made it to the back room she notice a safe sitting in a corner of the room, she begin to wonder what was in the safe.

But soon her mind switched to Faye and the food Faye was preparing.

Nancy got herself together in one of the mirrors in the room. She went back to the front room to make sure nothing was left out of order. She sat down to the coffee table and crushed one of the rocks and emptied a quarter of the tobacco out of two of the cigarettes. One of the cocaine rocks was big enough to make two healthy and strong cocaine cigarettes. She knew that Faye liked to smoke juice joints. Then she gathered the rest of the dope off of the table, put the two loose joints in her cigarette pack and headed for the door.

Faye had her ribs off the grill, and was inside preparing her fish along with potato salad. Her door was unlocked so Nancy invited herself in.

"What's the deal girl, have ya'll hooked up?" Faye asked.

"He wants me to keep the place up, you know wash dishes, clothes stuff like that." Nancy calmly placed the two cocaine cigarettes on the table.

"I brought you something." Faye noticed the two juice joints and responded.

"Yeah, that's cool, I fixed you a plate."

They both sat down at the living room table. Faye then got up to go get the condiments. Mustard and hot sauce for the fried fish and mustard based bar b cue sauce for the tender ribs, along with two ice cold Guinness stouts to drink. Nancy put the fork into the potato salad, and let Faye know that it was very delicious.

Faye is very attractive and intelligent. She's an Alabama girl that had been the first in her family to go to college. Since migrating to the big city, she has always remained independent. She always maintained a job and paid her bills on time. Faye is what many would call a thick sister with the naturally big thighs and calves, small waist and a bodacious posterior. Her face is somewhat described as 'Deep sexual Beauty'.

Faye has been in the big city for six years, and was introduce to smoking juice joints by a friend who helped her to find a place and employment. The friend stressed to Faye that a quick way to lose everything you want and have is to smoke crack cocaine straight raw with Char Boy and a shooter or stem. The friend lit a cigarette laced with crack cocaine and passed it over to Faye to try, and it's been her drug of choice ever since.

Her friend also taught her the art of boosting, which is the first criminal element a smoker uses when he or she is out of money and crack to smoke. There are allot of petty theft charges on folks records due to crack-cocaine alone. Faye learned the technique of taking a few items to the register that cost about a dollar, while her big purse was loaded with 50 dollar steaks and 75 dollar tender loin. She'd easily push her buggy out of the store that carried her purse filled with the boosted items. She got caught a few times that's what made her give that resort up.

After Faye and Nancy had finished their Q and fish Nancy lit one of the juice joints she had rolled up over at Skip's house. You see to a user of crack cocaine- smoking crack laced with something is far better than smoking straight crack out of a glass tube with metal brillo as the filter.

M eanwhile Teresa had on a tight short skirt and a tight knit halter that auctioned off her plum sized nipples. And pair of clogs that invited sex.

You know there is something about a woman, the beauty they posses. As an old man told me once, just look at the figure of any woman and you'll know that there is a God. "Man all of them are beautiful"! He would often say.

Teresa was just standing on the block, which is the entrance to the local merchant seaman hall. There was a guy that drove by and blew the horn. Teresa waived to the guy as he turned the nearest corner and circled back around. He got to the street Teresa was standing on and pulled up beside her.

"What's happening?" The driver asked.
"Aint nothing…what's happening?" Teresa responded.
"You want to make some money? He gestured for her to get inside of the car.
He opened the car door; Teresa got in and closed the door.
"O.K. baby girl, you got a stride?" Teresa didn't quite know what the guy was asking.

"You see baby, I've got these checks, and all I need for you to do is get one cashed. I'll peel you off nice, just cash this one. It's for forty-five hundred dollars. I'll give you a thousand if you bust this one for me.

But you got to have your stride or I.D. The banks are open now…Oh I'm Fred, nice to meet you, what's your name?"

"I'm Teresa." She continued. "So what you're telling me is that all I have to do is walk in the bank, give the teller my I. D. and social security card, and they'll cash the check?"

"Yeah."

"Let's go." She stated smooth and unabashed.

They arrived at the bank. Teresa swiftly stepped out of the car, walks inside of the bank, and walked over to one of the tellers, and presented the check. The teller looked closely at the check, and then she observed Teresa's ID's.

"How would you like this," asked the teller.

Teresa surprised and shocked paused for a second and responded, "It doesn't matter."

The teller gave Teresa back her ID's, opened the drawer and proceeded to count out four thousand-four hundred ninety dollars. Ten dollars were taken out for the cashing fee. Teresa grabbed the cash and didn't hesitate on leaving the bank. She quickly spotted Fred parked in the rear of the bank. She got into the car and signaled that she had gotten the cash. They quickly drove onto a busy thoroughfare and headed to the south side of town. Fred pulled into a middle school parking lot, and Teresa discreetly gave him the cash.

Fred then counted Teresa off thirteen hundred dollars. She was so surprised that the little scheme worked, and was shock over the cash she was looking at, she started perspiring.

"I'm going over here and get some dope from my mans…you smoke?"

"Yeah!" She answered excitedly, but tried to look cool.

"Well we can go over there and get some of that tension, get a room and smoke out."

The suggestion was paradise to Teresa.

She quickly admitted that she wanted to get something to smoke also.

"Cool," responded Fred. "I'll just call my mans… he has some drop and weight.

"Bet," Teresa responded.

They slowly pulled into a nearby Exxon to make the call. While Fred went to the phone booth to make the call, Teresa went into the store to purchase a sandwich, soda, four glass roses (crack stems), char buoy, a carton of cigarettes and a pack of lighters.

While Teresa was getting back into the car; Fred was still on the phone.

"Hello", the dealer answered.
"Yeah man, this Fred, you got any of those blocks?"
"Yeah, I got some of that fresh shit right now…how much you spending?
"Bout two-thousand," Fred said.
"I got you, come through," the dealer quickly said.
"I'm on my way."
Fred gets a block away from the dealer's residence; he fired up a Port and parked two houses down from where the dealer stayed. He told to Teresa to be cool and don't get out of the vehicle for nothing and that he'll only be a couple of minutes.
Fred got out of the car and headed to the dealer's front door, he knocked.

"Come on in Man… what's been happening?" Fred asked.
"Not a damn thing, looking at these silly ass niggers on the news shooting and killing each other every night…getting caught at nineteen years of age and got to do a thirty-year bid, that's about it man" The Dealer expressed.

"There it is there, right there my nigga." said the Dealer, referring to the block of cooked crack that laid on the coffee table.

Fred reached for the dope while handing the dealer Two thousand dollars. Fred picked up the dope from off the table, and then waited for the dealer to count the money while he walked slowly to the door.

"Appreciate this," Fred said as he left the house to get into his car. Fred slowly walked to the car. He placed the dope in the backseat and cranked up the car. For some reason, Teresa started doing a bunch of talking, asked to see the package and singing some type song that was aggravating the shit out of Fred.

"Look here man; you know what we got on us?" Fred ardently asked her.

Teresa didn't hear him rolling her window down singing the agitating song. Fred had gotten pissed and said.

"Bitch I got about 2 thousand dollars worth of crack in this car! Roll that window back up and stop all of that front street shit, or for God help me, I'll put your motherfucking ass out, right here!"

Teresa looked at him. And saw aggravation and blood was in Fred's eyes as she proceeded to let up the window and shut the fuck up.

"I'll let you see the package but let's get the fuck away from here, shiiit. Police live in this neighborhood; you don't see that squad car in that driveway?" Fred paused and continued. "Hey I apologize for that, but bitch I'm already illegal why should I invite a motherfucker to come and stop me...damn just be cool." He continued.

"We're on our way, we just took care of the biggest part, we got the crack. Just wait until we get to the hotel, it's hot as hell round here."

Teresa then sat back silently and fired up another Newport. They arrived at the Best Western on the south side. They get out of the car as Fred locked both doors with an automatic locking devise. Then they headed for the receptionist desk. Fred opened the door for Teresa as they both walked to the desk.

"Ah yes, I would like to have a room... preferably in the back of the hotel." Fred demanded.

The oriental receptionist was very attractive, and she stated that the rooms were eighty-two dollars a night.

"How many days would you like to have the room for Sir?" asked the receptionist. "And will you need a wakeup call."

"One day and No wake-up call," Fred answered.

"They received the key to the room and drove around to it. They put all of the crack and paraphernalia in a bag along with the sandwich, cigarettes and soda. They then stepped inside of the room.

"Damn this shit is nice," Teresa said referring to how nice of a room it was.

Fred turned on the TV and squeezed Teresa between her ass, while she told him she needed to get a shower. She got undressed in front of the mirror while Fred sat on the bed getting the crack stems ready. She cut the warm shower on and lathered up. She had braids but since she hadn't felt decent water or soap in a couple of days, she nearly emptied the lil bottle of shampoo into her scalp.

When she finished showering, she wrapped herself in a large towel, her hair was drying in another. Teresa then walked over and reclined in the bed while Fred brought the loaded crack stem to her. He then instructed her to tap on it (smoke it slowly).

"Yo man, I know how to chief this shit, just give me one of those lighters." Teresa stated adamantly.

Teresa struck the lighter; put the flame to the tip of the stem. A large cloud of smoke streamed through the stem- Teresa moved back quickly- stood up and placed herself on the bed on all fours, bending over with her ass up, she looked over her shoulder and told Fred rather quickly.

"Suck my pussy from the back while I take me a mega-blast."

Fred passed her a large piece of dope and Teresa puffed and pulled. The bite of the tension was incredible as she dropped the stem and the lighter onto a dry towel on the floor. She let the smoke out of her nose as Fred attacked both of her orifices from the back with his tongue.

Ahh motherfuckah…Damn, shit nigga! She exclaimed to Fred's cunnilingus technique.

Soon they both were naked and exchanging sexual favors- but what Teresa didn't know was that Fred was HIV positive. You see this guy that Teresa was now exchanging sexual favors with was infected with the virus that causes AIDS. Fred attracted the virus from a needle he shared once with a female who has full blown aids. They continued their unprotected sexual escapade, the potency of the crack had took away all their balanced judgment.

Teresa lay on the bed dazed, sweaty from all of the crack smoking and sexual activity.

"Damn that shit is some fire, I just want to smoke and relax now," Teresa pleasurably remarked. As she took another hit of the dope that laid on the bedside table.

The dope had tension and she was thinking about Judy.

"Yeah, we need to go pick up my girl Judy over there on Gum Street." Teresa stated.

"Oh yeah, first let me put this shit up that I put up under the mattress."

Fred removes the crack from beneath the mattress, puts it on the dresser and goes to the bathroom to wash up, as Teresa sat on the edge of the bed with her panties on, she took another blast, then she got up and put on her skirt and shoes.

"Yeah before we get to move anywhere I got to go to that mall and pick up me a nice outfit." Teresa stated.

As she slowly walked over to the dresser to get her purse- she opened it and counted nine hundred thirty-four dollars and some change. Fred returned from the bathroom fully dressed and grabbed the plastic bag full of dope and slid it in his waistband as he and Teresa headed for the door. On their way to the car they lit a cigarette, got into the car and pulled out of the parking lot and headed for the nearest mall to get Teresa's outfit.

"Damn I'm hungry," Fred remarked.

"There is a Seafood buffet near the mall, let's go there to eat because I'm kind of hungry myself. After we eat then we can go get the outfits, if that's what you want to do."

"I'm with it," Fred remarked.

They pulled into the buffet's parking lot; it must've been about seven p.m. The buffet had all of the lobster and raw oysters on the half-shell you can eat. The place wasn't crowded and they were seated rather quickly.

The waitress asked what will they be having. Fred said the buffet and sweet iced tea. Teresa said that she'll have the sprite. The waitress then brought plates and drinks over to them. Teresa and Fred then headed for the aisles of assorted seafood and desserts. While sitting at the table with crawfish, shrimp and lobster, Teresa asked Fred what were his plans for the checks.

"Well I need someone else, maybe your friend," Fred stated.

"Who, Judy?" Teresa asked.

"Yeah, there's a little liquor store that stays open until twelve tonight... they'll cash it. I have one for three thousand-six. Besides I'm tired of stepping to those banks," Fred said.

"This shit is safe isn't it, I mean this shit isn't going to come back to haunt me will it?" Teresa asked as she consumed the tasty seafood that was on her plate.

"Nah, it's cool I've been doing this shit for a few years now, nothing has happened yet, it's cool though."

Meanwhile back at Skip's place, Nancy's new residence. Skip is discussing a matter in his bedroom. He mentioned to Nancy that he would need for her to stay close to this special cell phone he'd just purchased. He was stating to Nancy about this meeting he was about to attend with a very prominent drug lord from Columbia, South America.

The meeting was highly confidential and he needed for her to be by the phone so that she could jot down some information- pen, paper, recorders or any other type of devise was not allowed in the meeting. Nancy took the phone, and asked Skip what time he was calling.

"Around about 9:30...an hour and a half from now," Skip continued, "I need for you to do this, this shit is important." Skip grabbed his keys and got into a white SUV and headed for the gentleman's club where he would get all of the information about the big connection. The mayor was already there, he was secretly let into the back entrance of the club, then led up to a VIP section of the club where the Colombian was sitting at a table dressed with wine and cheese...along with a saucer of uncut powdered cocaine... And finally accompanying them in the room was five of the thickest, sumptuous women known to the human eye. There was an East Indian beauty, a black goddess, an oriental, a white beauty and another black goddess from England.

The music thumped from the club while Skip parked at the back entrance. He later gave a coded signaled knock at the door and was quietly let in. Skip soon joined the two men at the table, where he and the Colombian were introduced by the mayor. The meeting started. The Colombian had a portable DVD player at the table where the screen was in sight for Skip and the Mayor to view. Both were silent and attentive when the Colombian spoke.

"I have a visual, I would like for you gentleman to take into consideration." Then he hit play on the remote.

The picture was very clear on the screen, and it showed the manufacturing process of cocaine from the Coca leaves to the packing of the substance and the shipping of it to America and around the world. Also shown was what this particular cartel does to fuck-ups or those who link government investigators to their organization. And what was viewed were twelve men, lined up against a wall, bound and tied up then each was brutally shot in the back of the head.

The Colombian shut off the DVD closed the player and said,

"It's a pleasure doing business with you gentlemen. "He took a sip of wine and got up-leaving a gold briefcase on the table.

Skip pulled out his phone because he had specific instructions to follow which were given to him at another part of the club by another member of the cartel. Skip began to call Nancy who was now smoking up the cooked up crack that was in Skip's dresser drawer. The drawer was carelessly neglected by Skip; he must have thought he put the drugs in the safe. The ring of the phone was muffled out by the sofa cushions. The phone ranged and ranged while the man was giving Skip the specifics about the deal.

Nancy was in heaven, taking hit after hit as the phone was now on its tenth ring. She was totally blinded and caught in the crack web. Nancy couldn't put the stem down as she sat on the side of the bed and puffed (smoked) devotionally.

Skip disconnected and caught the last part of the instructions from the Colombian. As the Colombian walked away- Skip dreaded the thought of asking the Colombian to repeat himself. He deeply regretted being involved with the entire situation and all he could think about were the instructions given to him that he clearly didn't get.

What was said to Skip by the Colombian was what to do with the money, the pay off instructions, what bank to deposit the money into and the account number. And none of the information was recorded by Skip in any way. He was hoping for Nancy to be by the phone to jot the instructions down, but she was caught in the 'Crack Spell.'

All the while, Fred and Teresa had been to the mall and were on their way to Judy's house.

"How far do we have to go?" Fred asked.

"Not far, just around the corner," Teresa responded.

Fred pulled up in front of Judy's house. Teresa got out of the car and mentioned to Fred that she would be back in a couple of minutes. Teresa knocks on the door as Judy peers through the glass opening of the door, to see who it was. Judy opened the door after recognizing that it was Teresa.

"Yeah what's up girl?" Judy asked, letting Teresa in and closing the door. They both sat on the couch. Judy's daughters had been asleep for awhile so she didn't bother awaking them. Teresa then pulled out a wad of cash, slammed it down on the coffee table and lit a Newport. Judy shocked of seeing the wad that was slammed on the coffee table asked Teresa what was up with it.

"Girl this dude I met today asked me to cash a check for him...Oh I apologize".

Teresa pulled out a stem she had pack with about fifty dollars worth of crack melted in it. She then handed Judy the stem, Judy grabbed the lighter that was laying on the coffee table-put the stem to her mouth and took a monster blast. Teresa then leaned over to Judy and cupped her breast and squeezed them softly- while saying quietly.

"C'mon girl it's more where that came from. Get your wallet with your ID. and let's go...C'mon!" Teresa continued, "See Nancy with that

bullshit, I don't play games. I was going to help you fuck that bitch up."
Teresa said as Judy put on her shoes, and headed for the door. Judy paused,
took a step back and told Teresa that they'll have to go get a money order
and drop the money in the drop box at the electric company.

"I'll need some food for my babies also; they are in their room
sleeping. I can't be long, because they're in house by themselves."

"We'll be back shortly," said Teresa, reassuring Judy that her two
girls that were asleep would be o.k. As they got into the car there was
a small introduction.

"Judy, this Fred, Fred this is Judy," Teresa said. She continued, "She
needs to get $150 money order for her electricity." Teresa said as she took
herself a hit off of the loaded crack pipe.

"Alright we can take care of that at that store we're headed to. Hurry
up, get in the car we can't be doing all that wild shit and do business at
the same time." He continued, "So all of the smoking and talking loud
keep it a little down until we've finish handling business, nice to meet
you young lady, I'm Fred." "I'm Judy, nice to meet you." As they took
off down the road.

"Where's the check? Teresa asked.

"Hey look here, slow your hype ass down! I've got enough illegal shit
in here that'll get all of us death row, so slow your ass down!"

He looked in the rearview mirror and started speaking with Judy.
I'll be quick, all you have to do is go into this little liquor store and
get the check cashed, you can get your bill money out of that." Fred
stated.

He then handed the check over to Judy; the check was for three
thousand - six dollars. Teresa then handed Judy a pint of Seagram's Gin
to get the geek off of her from that hit she took in the house. Judy took
a huge gulp and said, "I'm with it."

As Fred continued driving Teresa handed Judy a twenty- five dollar
piece of crack to the back seat, as Judy mounted the fat rock on the
stem and lit it...one could hear the dangerous crackle and sizzle of the
cocaine being heated, and as Judy placed the lighter and stem in the
cigarette holder inside of the car door Fred quietly said,

"C'mon baby now, get yourself together we got to get this money first, then we can smoke up Peru. Yeah, we're about to arrive at the store now, and here, drank you a little bit of this liquor before you go in," Fred suggested. As they pulled up to the corner, a block away from the store, Judy took another swig of the liquor.

"What I'm going to do is drop you off, and we're going to circle the block. When you have cashed the check, come out, and walk along the street and I'll pick you up, alright babe?" He stated to Judy.

"Alright," Judy answered as she got out of the car.

She then headed for the store's entrance and entered the store. The store's cahier noticed her but didn't pay her any attention. Judy then headed for the Cognac section of the store, with a small shopping cart in front of her. As she strode the aisles she grabbed a fifth of Hennessey, a half gallon of orange juice and a bottle of grey goose. When she put the items on the counter there was a customer ahead of her, so she picked up a Jet magazine and started reading it.

"Thank you, and give me a stick of that double mint gum," The customer stated to the cashier. The customer that was ahead of Judy paid for the gum and the other items and headed out of the store. Judy then stepped to the register, and put her items on the counter.

As the cashier scanned the first item, Judy started signing the back of the check and pulled out her social security card and photo ID. She then handed the cashier the check along with her ID's. The cashier briefly looked over the check and noticed the name of the company that the check was under, it was UK Ress one of the fraudulent check names on the list.

The cashier had finished ringing up Judy's items. Tammy, the cashier asked Judy to wait a minute, to see if the store had the funds. The cashier then went inside a little office behind the register, and called an officer that had been investigating the circulating of the bogus checks.

The cashier quickly stepped inside of the office behind the counter, which was concealed by window tint. She then dialed the investigating officer Ted Kollard, stating...

"Lieutenant, this is Tammy the owner of the Liquor store on 7th and Walnut. I have a female in this store now trying to cash one of those rubber checks." The lieutenant with pen and pad in hand asked what was written on the check, as she was beginning to tell him, she peeked her head briefly out of the of office and told Judy.

"I'll be with you shortly." Judy gave Tammy a relenting nod. The Lieutenant jotted down the information that was given to him, and the check read 'ELEGANT LIGERIE' INC, A UK RESS COMPANY. Tammy also gave the Lieutenant the description of the clothing Judy was wearing. The Lieutenant quickly gathered himself. He put on a bullet proof vest, strapped on his service revolver and headed out of the door.

Tammy then came out of the office and went to the counter to finish the transaction with Judy.

"Will that be all?"

"Oh and give me a money order for a hundred and fifty dollars."

Tammy bagged the items and counted off one thousand eight hundred and ninety-five dollars to her and thanked her. Judy grabbed the bagged items and left the store.

The time was then around 10:30 pm and Judy started to walk along Walnut Street. Lieutenant Kollard had already been parked at 8th and Medina behind some tall bushes. As Judy walked, Fred and Teresa pulled up beside her. Judy then discreetly got inside of the car's backseat.

"Damn girl you did it!" Teresa exclaimed noticing the bags that Judy had when she got into the backseat of the car.

"Yeah girl, I was kind of nervous, but I stayed cool." As she handed Fred the cash there was a flashing squad car behind them.

"Got damn the BABYLON!" Fred said of the police's squad car that followed him.

He grabbed the crack and stem away from Teresa and put it in the door of the car. Fred calmly pulled to the side, as the Lieutenant got out of the squad car and walked toward Fred's car to question him. Fred proceeded to roll his window down. The Lieutenant ordered Fred to step out of the car and for everyone in the car to keep still. Two more squad cars pulled up while the Lieutenant questioned Fred.

As the two officers approached the Lieutenant, one male officer and the other female. The Lieutenant told the two officers that there were two females in the vehicle. Each officer quickly went to the other side of the car to question Teresa and Judy.

"For my safety son I'd like to put these cuffs on you," said the Lieutenant. Fred cooperated with no struggle; the other officers cuffed Teresa and Judy as well.

"I believe these three have just cashed one of those bogus checks we've been trying to find." The lieutenant said to the officers, as they were putting the now cuffed Judy and Teresa in one of the squad cars along with the items that were purchased at the liquor store.

"I believe I know what's going on here, let's carry them back down to that liquor store," the lieutenant said. As they were pulling into the parking lot Judy started verbally assaulting Teresa.

"Motherfucker, got me out here on some bullshit, I can't believe this shit!" Judy exclaimed angrily. Teresa just sat there looking silently embarrassed. The Lieutenant let Fred out and the female officer led Teresa and Judy back in the liquor store, with the items that were purchased.

The Lieutenant asked Tammy, the owner and cashier of the liquor store, which female cashed the check. Tammy immediately pointed at Judy, Tammy continued on- "Lieutenant I have this entire transaction on tape…the time of the purchase, and the items, along with the cashing of the check."

"Excuse me Lieutenant, I have to lock this store up," Tammy stated, as she switched on a 'Closed' neon light in the store's front window. Tammy stepped behind the counter and retrieved the wireless monitor from out of the small office. She then put the monitor on the counter for the suspects and the officers to view. Tammy the store's owner came to the exact portion of the tape when Judy was at the counter cashing the check. The lieutenant asked Judy if that was her. Judy then looked at Teresa as if she wanted to murder her. One of the officers started removing the items from the bag. As the cloud of crack smoke started to leave Judy's mind she retorted.

"They gave me the check, these two motherfuckahs came around my house about an hour ago to get me to cash that check for them… my two babies are home alone as we speak."

The Lieutenant looked as if shocked, that her children were home alone at that time of the night. The Lieutenant switched his attention on the children and told the officer to take Teresa and Fred to the station and book them.

"I'll personally handle the matter with her getting to those kids, ya'll take those two down to the station- Ms. Tammy I think I've seen all I need to see, and I have your number. Let's get them up out of here and down to the station," the Lieutenant said.

As they all departed he asked Judy where she stayed.

"The address is on my ID," said Judy.

"Ma'am look here this is not a time to get smart, I could have easily had your ass hauled down the station with those other two…now what's your address?!"

"It's 27 Gum Street." Judy answered rather snobbishly.

"Is there a relative I can take them to, until this matter is resolved?" The Lieutenant asked.

"Yes, my sister Lisa, she lives at 555 Brideir, motherfucking basers!" Judy cried out, with tears falling from her eyes.

While the Lieutenant and Judy were on their way to get the kids he tried to make her feel relaxed.

"We've been trying to catch this guy for months and finally we have him. There is a chance you won't be charged with anything just tell me the entire story when we get to the precinct."

As they arrived at the front door of Judy's house, the lieutenant turned off the car and stated to Judy that it would be more convenient if she was un-cuffed.

"If you run, it's only going to make it worse for you and your children… got me?"

"Yes," Judy answered very humbly as she got out of the passenger side of the squad car and the Lieutenant got out of his side. They entered the house. As soon as they stepped into the house Judy headed for the girl's room and found them sound asleep. She woke the girls up and told them that they were going to they're Aunt Lisa's house. As Judy was packing her daughters' clothing, she called for the Lieutenant. The Lieutenant stepped to the entrance of the room, as Judy gave him her sister's Lisa phone number. She finished packing the children's clothing, the lieutenant dialed Lisa's number from his cell phone in the living room.

"Hello." Lisa answered.

"Ah, yes ma'am, this is Lieutenant Kollard from the police department. I have your sister Judy in custody she's alright though." He continued. "I just need to take her down to the station for questioning"

"One more thing Lisa."

"What's that Lieutenant?"

"I would appreciate it, if you could take care of her daughters until all of this is over."

"Bring them over!" Lisa adamantly exclaimed.

"We will do that Lisa." As they were headed out of the door, the Lieutenant asked the girl's how do they feel about going over to Aunt Lisa's house, they responded positively, but with no great adulation because they had been just awaken from a deep sleep. The Lieutenant just smiled.

"You seem to have a nice relationship with your sister."

"Yes, we've always been close and we'll always be close and look out for each other sir. It was just us and our mother, we vowed as little girls to always do for each other."

The Lieutenant just looked at her with a deep feeling of admiration, because he is not that close to own blood. They engaged in small talk while the little girls, one in the back the other in the front seat, went back to sleep. As they pulled up to Lisa's house, the Lieutenant parked and blew the horn Lisa opened her door while Judy walked the girls up to the door to say her good byes.

Lisa, saying not a word let the girls in and told them to go to bed, in the room that they sleep in when they come to visit her. Lisa, being the older of the two and knowing the gravity of the matter, didn't get in to much wordage with her little sister; she just kissed Judy on the cheek and told her to call whenever she gets the chance.

As Judy and the Lieutenant were headed down to the police station; they engaged in a bit of dialogue.

"So what do you think about all of this senseless killing that's going on around this city?" The Lieutenant asked. The crack cloud was still dancing in her head along with the bad feeling of being arrested so she didn't have too much to say. The lieutenant responded,

"I don't know, well I think it goes back to parenting, when I was being raised, every adult in your neighborhood had the right to chastise you. I personally think it has a great deal to do with how we discipline our children these days. Back when I was growing up if I did something I was not supposed to be doing and the neighbor saw me doing it, that adult neighbor chastised me and when she told my mama, she whipped my ass again when she had gotten in from work."

The Lieutenant continued. "Now days, if the mother disciplines or spank the child she gave birth to, she stands a chance of going to jail or getting in trouble with CPS(Child Protective services), and that bullshit about 'Time Out' and go to your naughty chair, the naughty chair is going to be my fist in their Got damn chest. I don't have time to wrestle and play with something I feed and clothe. That's a fool." The lieutenant explained as he continued. "My mother didn't kill me when she was whipping my behind. Instead it taught me right from wrong and not to do those bad things I was caught doing. These parents better wake -up, because when their offspring grows up, prison or the grave is going to be their discipline, and there is no naughty chair in any of those places."

Judy just nodded her head in acquiesce as they pulled into the booking area of the police station. Fred and Teresa had already been booked, photographed and fingerprinted.

Meanwhile Nancy was at Faye's house smoking up Skip's dope and getting sexually gratified at the same time. The two were in one of Faye's rooms. Nancy was in a rather suggestive sexual position, being orally stimulated by Faye while they were heavily smoking. Skip had come home from that meeting and he was looking for Nancy and she wasn't there. He searched every room in his house then he thought that she might be over to Faye's across the street.

Skipped walked outside and looked across the street and decided to go ask Faye if she'd seen Nancy. As he approached the door's entrance to Faye's house he started to hear deep moans and grunts coming from one of windows on one side of Faye's house. He decided to turn the knob of the door which was unlocked and stepped in, the moans and grunts of the two ladies pleasing each other were louder and clearer now. Skipped decided to tiptoe to the room where the noise was coming from. He peeped through the door and discovered Nancy and Faye naked in Faye's king size bed.

Skip burst through the door raging mad. He quickly went after Nancy, disregarding Faye. He beat Nancy repeatedly in the face, blood was everywhere and all Faye could do was listen to Nancy's cries of great pain and fear as she escaped her house, wearing nothing but a gown and cell phone, she hurriedly dialed 911. The dispatcher at the police department retrieved the 911 call.

"911, may I help you?" The dispatcher asked. Faye paused with shocking hesitance, then said,

"Yes, there has been a brutal beating on Gum Street. Five-forty Gum Street.

Please hurry!" exclaimed Faye, as she walked further away from the house…towards a well lit intersection. After about five minutes a cop noticed her, as she waived him down. The officer then approached her with the windows down.

"Sir, my friend is being beaten badly, by this guy Skip that lives across the street from me."

"Get in ma'am.", responded the officer.

As they approached Faye's house, which was five houses down from the intersection- Nancy was crawling outside on Faye's front porch near the top stair as if she was hanging on to her last breath. Her forehead was gashed open as the blood poured down her two black and swollen eyes, which joined the other gashes and blood all over her naked body. They both got out of the squad car. Faye ran over to comfort her brutally beaten friend. The officer slowly moved Faye away and sent signals out to emergency rescue and more police officers.

The EMTs and officers arrived at the repugnant scene. The emergency technicians carefully placed Nancy on the stretcher. While she was being place inside of the Rescue truck, the officer begins to get information from her, as best as he could.

"Ma'am, who did this to you?"

"Skip, his real name is Trevor Karp," Faye spoke up loud for her friend, who couldn't mutter a word. She continued. "He's driving a white 2004 Chevy Blazer." Nancy then closed her eyes for a moment, as Faye looked long at her friend as the doors closed on the rescue truck.

Faye went inside of her house to get dressed, and headed to the hospital. All the while, the officers and evidence technicians were inside of Skip's place looking for any trace of him. One of the officers discovered the safe, which was loaded with drugs, money and a 3 and a 1/2 foot Burmese python. Also a couple of guns were lying on the dresser in the room, one of the officers then brought it to the attention of the other officers.

As the officers were confiscating Skip's drugs and guns. The captain called in the evidence technicians to collect the fingerprints on the safe. After all of the evidence was collected. The captain then decided to cut into the safe.

"Let's get this safe open, now!" The captain shouted.

Within minutes the officers had the safe open and out slithered a vexed python. One of officers tazed the snake, while another officer filled it with 2 bullets from his service revolver.

"Damn what's this shit?" Shouted one of the officers as the captain reached inside to expose more of the contents that were inside the safe. Contents as: Old school hip-hop gold and platinum ropes and nameplates, a brown bag full of gold, platinum and diamonded cut partial teeth-fronts, along with an un-estimated amount of cash and two large zip lock bags of cooked crack cocaine. One of the bags contained dimes and twenty cent blocks, and the other bag was filled with slabs, cookies and pies.

"Man, this guy is the real deal," One of the officers said.

"I believe so, I believe so," The captain said.

At that time the captain put out an APB for a black male driving a white 2004 Chevy Blazer.

Faye explained to the Captain that Marcy Nixon is a good associate of Skip, and that she usually buys crack from him from time to time. Faye calls Marcy on her cell phone.

"Hello," Marcy answered.

"Yea this is Faye. Skip has nearly killed Nancy. I have the police here and they would like to speak with you. Girl, Nancy is fucked up bad girl, try to help us out." Faye explained, then she handed the captain the phone.

"Hello".

"Hello Ms. Nixon, how are you?"

"I'm alright, thank you."

"Yes, Ms. Nixon we would appreciate it, if you would help us apprehend Mr. Trevor Karp, you know him as Skip."

"Yes". Marcy responded.

"Well he's wanted; he's assaulted Ms. Nancy Taylor very badly." The captain calmly expressed.

"OK, I usually call a 728 number when I want to get in touch with him."

Marcy explained.

"Yes that's the number that I have. Ma'am, get a pen and paper. His number is 728-3626. Call that number and tell him that you would like to spend some time with him, anything he's very desperate right now and is looking for a place to hide. When he decides to come quickly dial 55 pound and we will handle it from there. You will not be harmed when we arrive at your home, we will shine a bright light inside of your front window. That would be the signal for you to move away from him, like in another part of your house, because we're knocking down the door....it will be done quickly ma'am, no need to fret. What is your address ma'am?"

"6991 North Jax Avenue," Marcy responded."

"Yes, we will be there shortly…and remember to dial 55 pound when he arrives. Oh and Ms. Nixon, we apologized for bothering you." The Captain stated.

"Alright captain, it's not a problem… I'm happy to assist." Marcy stated as she hung up the phone.

All the while, back at the police station. Judy and the lieutenant were getting out of his squad car to have her booked and processed. Fred and Teresa were already in jail, garbed and waiting in holding cells. Fred was put into the male holding cell, while his two female accomplices were put into a female holding cell. All three were individually questioned- Fred was called out of the cell to be questioned first. Two officers were in the interrogation room sitting a at a five-foot by three foot wide metal table- surrounded by four metal chairs. Fred was seated across from the two officers.

"Where did you get the checks from?"

"What are you talking about? ... I don't know about no damn checks man." Fred adamantly answered.

"Your fingerprints are all over those checks dating back three to four months ago. Sir, you are neither affiliated nor work for any of those companies, can you explain that?" The officer questioned.

Fred looked at the captain with a look of dexterity and confidence on his face.

"I did some side work for the president of the company," Fred retorted.

"Oh yeah, what type of work did you do?"

"I did a little painting, some yard work, hauling garbage- things like that."

"Well, we're in luck sir, because I happen to have the phone number of the owner the Siloam Company." One of the interrogating officers stated.

He then proceeded to call the owner. It was mid-morning around 3 am, and the owner Mr. U.K. Ress, had given Captain Tuc (short for Tuchanchevsky) the green light on alerting him as soon as they capture the person who had been stealing the checks to his company.

The phone ranged once.

"Hello," answered Mr. Ress.

"Mr. Ress this is Captain Tuchanchevsky of the Police Department. Sir, I believe we have the man who's been stealing and cashing your companies checks, right here in our custody. All you have to do is come down to the station and sign a few documents to prosecute. The entire process will only take about 30 minutes." He continued.

"Anyway Mr. Ress, have you ever heard of a Fred Biggs, he claims he's done some work for you."

"Nah, never heard of him, I have few employees and I know the names of all of them."

"Alright thank you sir, you can come down anytime preferably this morning sir, the faster you can get here to do these papers the faster it would be to put this guy away."

"I got you Captain, will do, and thanks."

As they both hung up the phone, Captain Tuc continued on interrogating Fred.

"Got some bad news. That man said he's never heard of you, I guess you can explain it to the Judge."

The Captain signaled to the other officer, to get Fred out of there. They questioned Teresa and got her statement. Judy spoke against both of them. Making a case about her girls being asleep and Teresa and Fred picking her up to do the caper.

The lieutenant spoke in Judy's behalf. He made his way into the interrogation room to speak with the Captain.

"Captain that young lady Judy Vial is innocent; I think she was just going for the ride." He continued, "She is willing to testify against the other two that got her in this mess."

"Yeah, we'll play it by ear for now. Go home and get some rest man."

The Lieutenant whispered something to the Captain before leaving the room.

"Judy Vial is innocent. Captain, if you would… show her little sympathy if possible.

The Captain looked the Lieutenant squarely in the eye, and said,

"I received message from the technician's lab and her fingerprints are over all of the drug paraphernalia and drugs that were in that car. There was enough crack in that car to get an entire city block high. I'll have to think closely on that, but I respect your judgment Lieutenant. Now go on home and get some rest." The Captain stated.

On his way out of leaving the station the Lieutenant passed by the holding cell and took a long look at Judy. Judy made eye contact with him as he gestured to her with his right thumb up, that everything was going to be all right. Judy exchanged the glance of the Lieutenant while sitting on one of the holding cell benches. Drops of tears escaped Judy's eyes then rolled down her cheeks. The Lieutenant then left the station and headed home.

"Hello, somebody paged me?" Skip question Marcy who had called him earlier but he had his ringer off. His cell was on vibrate, stuffed into one of his seats.

"Yeah Skip this Marcy, I need something."

"Yeah what's up, you aint talked to no Babylon in the last hour, have you?" Skip questioned her.

"Fuck nigga- what the fuck you coming from. I need some dope, and you up here bullshitting! Where you at man?" Marcy asked Skip.

"I'm on Beach One Boulevard right now. I'm in your neighborhood." Skip replied.

"Nigga this me… I aint with none of that! I need a two -hundred dollar brick and if your game is tight enough nigga…I might let you suck on some of this Fat pussy."

Not wanting to stay out in the streets to long, Skip put up with the verbal onslaught displayed by Marcy, and calmly stated.

"I'll be there bitch." He stated then closed his cell.

Meanwhile back at the police station it was now morning. Fred, Teresa and Judy were making their first appearance in court. All three had their finger prints on the checks. The owner of the Siloam Company, Mr. U.K. Ress wanted each of them to be prosecuted to the fullest extent of the Law. The judge ran off the charges, forgery, Grand Larceny, Embezzlement, of a total of sixty-thousand dollars and stolen property.

"How do you plead?" The Judge stated.

"Not guilty," Fred pleaded.

Teresa and Judy pleaded the same. All three were then held in custody with no bond until their next court date.

W ho is it?" shouted Marcy as she came to her door.
"This Skip."

"Hold on", replied Marcy as she immediately dialed Captain Davis-
to alert him that Skip had made it to her house. Then closed the cell
phone and slipped it into the waist pocket of her gold, green, purple
and dominated by black traditional oriental thigh cut silk robe that
she wore. Her thick legs were covered by fully-fashioned, vintage black
nylon stockings with seams, a beige garter belt and corset with ankle
strapped heels- she looked very tantalizing indeed.

Her hour-glass thick figure put her in the class of 'Live Bitch'.
Along with her freshly done hair and manicured nails. Her make-up
was perfect and she exemplified the perfect functional crack smoker,
not a crack head …there is difference in the two terms, because there is
different behavior in the two abusers.

She opened the door for Skip. He stepped inside of the apartment
and immediately closed the door. Marcy knew he was in trouble so she
bothered not to question Skip's timorous and nervous behavior.

"Close the blinds, right there," ordered Skip, as he sat on the living
room sofa sweating.

"Nigga I aint with this shit, I want some crack!" Marcy said as she
closed her living room blinds, and then proceeded to walk to her linen
closet to retrieve a clean cotton hand towel for him to wipe his face with.

"What you drinking man?" Marcy asked, as she saw him cutting up
blocks of crack on her glass coffee table. She slowly walked behind the

bar and poured two straight glasses of chilled Navan Grand Marnier cognac, and brought the two filled glasses to the glass coffee table, laced with bricks of crack and powdered cocaine. She then bent over and clapped her ass cheeks slowly and loud. Then she turned around and retrieved a Pyrex glass stem that was in the cuff of the armrest in her sofa.

Marcy then coolly took her a sip of the Navan placed it back on the table and mounted her up about a thirty dollar brick. Marcy pulled on the dope slow and smoothly, while straddling skip's face with her now wet and succulent vagina and full cocoa shaded stocking covered thighs. Skip hungrily sucked Marcy's pussy as if he hadn't eaten or drunken anything in two or three months. Loud smacking and slurping noises were made as Marcy freely moved her delightfully tasty honey holes over Skip's osculating mouth.

"Uhh shit, ooh damn," were Marcy's explicit verbal expressions.

"Baby you like the way that pussy taste? Marcy sensuously asked. "Umm-hum," responded Skip.

As Marcy lit the tip of the Pyrex glass stem loaded with cocaine sap; she proceeded to inhale deep. The coke smoke transfixed her for a second as she withdrew her face away from the heavily smoked filled stem, and tossed the lighter and stem on the floor, as she continued to ride Skip's face she took a peek out of the window blinds. Marcy noticed that Captain Davis and about three squad cars were parked a distance away from her house.

Suddenly Skip started to realize his reason for being there. He lifted Marcy off of his face and said.

"Marcy, I'm in deep trouble." Marcy responded in calm and said to Skip, that he needs to hit the stem.

Skip who would never do such a thing, looked at her as if she had lost her mind, as he proceeded to sniff a 3 inch thick line of powdered cocaine and took a gulp of the Navan cognac.

"Nigga, you know I was supposed to cut you for that bullshit." She was referring to him pushing her off of his face.

"For real girl something happened and I need for you to know that. If I'm caught by anybody I'm going down. I need to stay here until this bullshit clears. I...I got to get out of state, you know far away from here, shit maybe out of the country," as he looked at her with a look of perplexity. Marcy gathered herself on the couch and looked at him with an understanding gaze, because she knew what was happening. Marcy and Nancy are close friends and Nancy's assaulter was sitting across from her. Skip on the other hand was thinking about his next move. He took a brief look out of the blinds and didn't see anything to get alarmed about. Everything looked normal, because the police had positioned themselves very inconspicuously.

At that time the lights flashed for a quick second through the window.

Marcy knew she needed to act fast, so she said to Skip- "I have a surprise for you." She accentuated as she rose to her feet.

"Surprise?... I don't need no fucking surprise. Sit down right here."

"Nigga you've got one more time to tell me what to do and not do in my mothafuckin house, just be glad pussy nigga- that you up in here."

Normally those two words brought death or a brutal confrontation to the person that said them, but Skip knew Marcy was always slick out of the mouth, so he paid it no mind. Instead took a card he had in his pocket and scooped up a Montana size toot of cocaine and sniffed it.

Aware that the cops were surrounded around her house ready to invade it… she sashayed to the back of the house. Feeling totally relaxed for now, Skip paid none of her actions any mind. He felt safe and away from the police…at least that's what he thought.

While Mazaratis' 'I Guess it's all Over' lowly sounded out of the speakers. Marcy went to one of the back rooms, and locked the door. She was waiting for the police to knock down her front door and apprehend Skip. Skip at this time continued to sniff powder and peek out of the blinds on occasion.

The police were already in position around the house, as Marcy waited in anticipation for the officers to break down the front door. Marcy quietly zoned out and thought deep about her friend Nancy. She was closer to Nancy than anyone. Nancy and Marcy went to grade school together. Marcy knew the real Nancy, not just the Nancy that wants to be a slick crack abuser.

As Skip comfortably sat on the couch- There was sudden loud blast as the officers flattened the door.

"Throw ya hands in the air," shouted one officer." Skip complied with their demands, while Marcy waited in that locked backroom waiting for all of it to be over, so she could get to the side of her nearly murdered friend.

Skip's hands were put behind his back as an officer cuffed him.

"Let's take this very easy man, and everything will be cool," demanded the officer.

The Captain entered the house, looked at Skip with an angry gaze and proceeded to look through the house for Marcy- as the officers took Skip out and put him in the back of one of the squad cars. Marcy has now put on a longer robe to cover her enticing beauty.

There was a knock at the back room door where she was waiting. Marcy opens the door; the Captain gives her a long embrace. And even though she's a little high, she manages to keep her composure. Marcy then tells the captain that she's got to get a drink.

"Sure ma'am," courteously stated the Captain.

The Captain and Marcy stepped to the font room. She poured herself a straight glass of Seagrams extra-dry gin. She took a couple of extra long gulps, and then lit a Newport short cigarette. The slow gin and cigarette took the geek off of her, she now felt calm- "How's my friend, is she alright?" Marcy asked.

The Captain pulled out his cell phone.

"I'm going to call the hospital now, but I would like to thank you for helping us in capturing that guy, thank you Ms. Nixon."

"No, problem, stated Marcy, as she took another drank of the gin.

The Captain then proceeded to dial the number to the hospital.

"City medical emergency room may I help you?" The receptionist said.

"Ahh yes, this is Captain Rollins Davis with the city police department," he continued, I would like to know the whereabouts of a Ms. Nancy Taylor.

"Yes Captain, she is on the Trauma Ward. She's in critical condition, but the doctor says that she's going to be fine. I was told to give you the information of her admitted room when she's stabilized, she'll be admitted to room 62 on the 6th floor. Sir, she's going to be fine."

"Well ma'am thank you," said the Captain and hung up the phone.

The Captain turned to Marcy and told her that Nancy was alright, that loosened up Marcy; hearing the news that her childhood friend would be okay.

"They have all of the information at city medical- Oh yeah, Mrs. Nixon, there's a reward for you down at the station. Fellas, ya'll get all of this dope out of this lady's house- yeah, get all that off of her coffee table and take it down to the station."

"Thank you Captain, quietly said Marcy."
"Ma'am if you need me, call me," the Captain said to Marcy as he was walking out of the door.
"Here's my card."
"I will," Marcy answered.

Marcy closed the door after everyone had left her house and sat on the couch, feeling a little dejected as she started to reminisce about her and Nancy's friendship. She finally took one more draw off of the cigarette and gathered her thoughts, then she showered got dressed and went to city medical.

Now Judy, Teresa and Fred went to trial. They were in front of a twelve member Jury- who were to decide each of their fates. The state had proven that Fred was guilty of stealing and cashing over sixty-thousand dollars of bogus and unauthorized company payroll checks, and was sentenced to twenty-two and a half years in the state penitentiary.

Teresa was also found guilty. Her finger prints and photos of her and Fred together a couple of times proved that she was very guilty in assisting him in cashing those bogus checks. Teresa was sentenced to serve sixteen years at a women's correctional facility. She was also diagnosed of having the virus, the virus that causes the AIDS disease. Teresa contacted the disease from Fred when only having a onetime unprotected sexual experience.

Judy was given a break due to her nonexistent criminal record, her two beautiful girls and a slew of letters written by her aunt and uncle. Also her sister Lisa wrote a stand up letter to the Judge. Judy was given five years probation and was ordered to attend NA (Narcotics Anonymous) meetings for six years straight.

Trevor 'Skip' Karp is now doing twenty-five to Life for attempted murder and drug trafficking.

Faye, Marcy and Nancy are doing well both are leaders in their NA home groups. All three are living clean from narcotics and alcohol, and they all attend NA and AA meetings religiously.

Tonya, who got out of selling drugs, is now working in the school board; she owns and lives in a marvelously spacious home along with her two children in a suburb outside of Atlanta, Georgia.

Stay tuned for the continuation of Crack Spell
after these few words from the Author...

It's a twenty-four hour a day job staying off of crack-cocaine. When you're home relaxing and there is nothing to do, that's when you have to be on guard for your life.

You're relaxing drinking a cold beer, you start to get slightly intoxicated and you decide to take it a step further. You go out and purchase a few pieces of crack and use them, that's when the hell starts. A recovering drug addict shouldn't drink any alcohol, because it really impairs the judgment. And that's why in the NA meetings they say stay away from all mind altering substances.

Complete abstinence from all mind altering substances is very necessary, if the drug addicted person wishes to be cured.

Most will say being addicted to crack cocaine is a mind thing, well if that is true; how does one change an addicted person form of thinking. I think the person should expel all negatives thoughts from the mind. Heavily crack addicted individuals must train themselves to think positive, and stay away from those that use at all cost.

Smoking crack keeps you broke. Some said they started smoking because they saw a friend mount up. This is to the young people- any person that you call a friend will never introduce you to use any form of illegal narcotic or street drug. The crack world is a wild world. This person told me once; he'll get paid, go to smoke his crack at a house with other addicts. When the guy had no money or drugs left, the owner of the house would tell this guy that he'd have to leave.

The guy had to leave when he no longer had drugs or money to supply the owner and others around the house. When the crack and money are gone so will the so called friends. You'll never have a good outcome from smoking crack, you'll only suffer lost...for real.

I would usually go downtown and see people hanging out at convenient stores, and gas stations no functional activity, just crack habits.

There is a verse in the bible that states: Come from among them and be ye separate, for what fellowship does light have with darkness. You can't have three weeks clean and hang around a bunch crack addicts.

An individual may have three weeks clean from alcohol and drugs, and some situation may come into their normal living that they can't handle: A broken relationship, an argument, conflicts of all sorts, or just being bored with life and the beautiful occurrences of clean living. An addict with clean time may internally deal with these occurrences in the form of smoking crack. A relapse has occurred. A relapse is when an individual has a certain amount of clean time and goes back to using drugs.

I know an ex-athlete, with a pride and mindset that an athlete has or anyone who had accomplished anything that's of significance these days. You never think that you could ever become addicted to anything, until you've smoked crack cocaine. When this person was addicted he would go everywhere for help and he might stay away from the drug a week or two and found himself going to his drug of choice, crack cocaine.

I'm letting the cat out of the bag, by admitting that this person was addicted to the drug, because for some reason it has always been Taboo to admit that, that drug had this person. While he was in use of the narcotic he would forget and neglect important shit he needed to take care of. If you are upwardly mobile and have goals you won't accomplish them...if you are smoking crack. And that's written in stone.

The time a person wasted in addiction to crack- cocaine has nothing to do with anyone, but themselves, and they get punished for it. When they look back on their life and see the valuable time they've wasted, they suddenly think to themselves, they would say; "Damn that shit consumed almost a hundred percent of my adult life, and I don't have a damn thing to show for it. There is old crack saying…"You're putting it all up in the air". And when the high and crack is gone you're stuck with you. The same immature person that started smoking the drug will be the same immature person when you decide to stop smoking.

In the crack game you'll pay dearly for the usage of it. You'd be consumed with "Oh I could've done this or that with the money," but the time and money has all gone up in smoke- setting your life on fire… somebody call the fire department. And that's the way of sobriety. You would stay clean when you tell yourself this: "I will be clean for myself, no 12 step program, but the program that I set for myself, not what some other individual printed up in a book. I've seen it where a guy went to jail for living out the eighth step of the AA book. He was admitting his wrong he'd done to this certain female and was trying to make amends after 8 years of the incident. Authorities got a hold of the matter, and he was taken to jail. Not taking anything away from meetings and doing the 12 step program, but you would have to have personal disciplined program and goals set for yourself. What you put into it, is what you would get out of it, keep trying to get sober and clean it's worth it.

In the day that we're living in, many and more people are experimenting with drugs and alcohol. Whether it's not fitting in a certain group or losing a good providing job, more new addicts are surfacing by the minute as you read this. Some will die in their addiction, and some will hit rock bottom and lose everything before they realize that cunning and baffling enemy known as crack, pills and alcohol, has put in work …destroyed them.

Crack forces you to lose everything, just for example: You could have nine hundred in the bank and smoke a dime of crack and the drug would demand that you go and buy more. That one little dime piece of crack will totally have you emptying out that bank account. Some that I know of, have went and bought groceries from the grocery store, sat in their living room with just a dime rock. They'd smoke that dime; spend whatever cash they had left from the grocery store, smoke that up. Then starts pulling groceries they'd just purchased out of the refrigerator and freezer to pawn for money or more crack.

The feeling that you get from smoking crack is like no other feeling you will ever experience. Crack stimulates the pleasure sensors in your brain, which gives you a pleasurable feeling when you smoke it. The crack high only last for about three to six minutes, depending on the grade of the crack-cocaine that's being smoked. And it comes with a shocking 'let down.' The come down off of crack-cocaine is called 'total desperation' or geeking and fiending, in other words you want and demand for more. All of your dignity and processions you will lose. The come down off the use of crack demands that you get more and nothing else. People will do insane things to get another hit; Pawn the car, sell the jewelry, steal and even kill for the drug.

If you are addicted to Crack-cocaine get help, and keep getting help!

It's a must for your life that you stay away from the use of this terrible and illegal narcotic. And on the half of staying clean it's possible to do that. It's a must that the recovering addict gets his or her life back. The recovering addict stays clean in one thing, and that's having love for self. The product crack-cocaine is so addictive and it's hard to quit, because the pleasure of smoking it is so great. To have a body culminating orgasm is the equivalent to taking a good blast of good crack; now that's addicting. But the difference is Cumming is free and crack is not. Cumming is natural pleasure, crack is artificial pleasure.

When your car and money, house and health are gone then that's a hell ending. Of course you feel good for a brief moment, but then the end result of using comes quickly, which is one of the most horrible feelings any human could ever experience. When you take that last blast and don't have any more to back it up, it feels like you're all alone in the cold Pacific Ocean with only a life preserver at 1 o'clock in the morning with nothing but Great White Sharks circling you…and that's real as you're looking at your hand right now.

Money is lost; the addict hates himself and others around him. They have hair trigger reactions to everything that offends them. Emotions are things that we all have to control and if we have trouble on getting the satisfaction we want mentally and physically then we can ask God in prayer. Yes we make decisions everyday to either enhance or diminish our well being, it's up to the individual. I got a partner that's close to me, he told me that some smoker who stayed with him in the little house they rented, removed the stove out of the house then sold it for a twenty... that's low. If you are addicted get help if you want to chill, and have good times in your life...whatever you do don't smoke that base... because using crack will demand your life.

The authorities knew what this drug was about before it became popular. They knew it would take lives, keep people unemployed suffering, one less person they would have to worry about and if you are weak minded on crack, then you are doing them a big favor; one less person to worry about. Getting that craving off your back is the key thing, and once it's off, keep praying and going to meetings, hang around people who are really trying to recover, and don't use. I hear people say that their best thinking got them in this position of becoming a slave for crack. Actually it's their worst thinking that got them there. I look at it like this. If you think constantly of being a success in life, that's what will happen to you. If you think of smoking the stem that's what can happen you; destruction.

Doing whatever in life requires actions and thought, remember what your people told you, "You can do anything you put your mind to, and staying clean is what an addicted individual should have on their mind.

A recovering drug addict has one thing daily to think about and that is how he or she will stay off of narcotics, particularly crack-cocaine. Most of the time money can be a trigger for going out to use or losing an important relationship, whether it be money or a relationship or anything, DON'T USE. A newly recovering addict should concentrate on abstaining from the narcotic and or damaging substances that's destroying his or her life. Purify yourself constantly, just doing whatever it takes to get clear of the hell smoking crack brings. To seek something greater for yourself and accepting the good that is the beginning of staying clean and sober; input God's power and graces in your repertoire for staying clean and sober, through prayer, it works.

This book is about getting clean and nothing else. Nothing but getting clean and staying clean off Crack, Meth, Alcohol, prescription pills such as Oxycotin, Roxycotin or whatever it maybe that's causing you damage in this life. The first week of sobriety maybe your strength, yes your first week may be the motivating factor for years even decades of sobriety. Work hard the first week on getting clean, surround yourself with people that are strong and clean, people that knows what it's like to give up the heavy burden of crack addiction.

Every strong impressive building has a strong foundation; the addict must have individuals in his or her life that knows what the person is going through. Everything has to have a base in order for it to become or be successful. Even the huge skyscrapers, all of the glass and steel that you see are supported with a base or foundation. Buildings stand for ions if they are supported by a strong base. We as the owners and rulers of existence must have a strong base if we're to sustain ourselves as well as others and things around us.

Protecting your property and mindset, 'Stay away from people places and things is a constant saying at NA and AA meetings and is definitely a building block or foundation to build upon. This one saying can sustain you for thirty days plus, but what I'm saying is that you have to have your own personal foundation or base to keep you clean from the damaging substances or mindsets. This personal base will sustain you; it acts as a barrier or a boundary that you will not pass. Before an individual is addicted to Crack or Meth they had no boundaries they were Gung-Ho open and accepting anything in their life whether it was good or bad.

When I was coming up, there were certain things that adults who had admiring possessions wouldn't do. I watch these things and paid close attention. They had boundaries, they worked, they paid bills, and they bought cars and took good care of their kids.

Crack, Meth or abusing alcohol wouldn't have allotted them to do these things. Just as today these crippling substances would not allow a healthy home to be run properly. The bottom line is having a base for your personal success, because no one gives a damn if you blow all of your loot on crack, meth or alcohol.

I've heard stories of people who don't use and I asked why haven't they tried crack, or abused alcohol- I received all types of responses, but the most intelligent one was when people would say "I saw how it did other people." They pictured the loss of possessions: cars, a home and the furniture, they saw how it had fucked up someone else's life; then avoided the pain. Many addicts smoke on impulse, the first impulse- without thinking out the consequences or what will be the end result of the activity of smoking crack or using alcohol. I know the end and it's one of the most challenging a person could ever face.

Lose everything- possessions, your body, mind etcetera, this is very serious. Crack demands that and more. That's why allot of older heads will tell you... "Man, you fuck with that, and you'll never have anything." That's all they'll say and walk off.

Some crack and Meth abusers are very intelligent people. I heard it once said that some are afraid of themselves and success. They tend to have this mindset of well even though I have this Bachelors degree, and can apply at any of these companies and land a job, I won't, because I've been in poverty for so long I wouldn't know how to react to living a respectable decent life. I'll just do crack and meth and choke my dreams. I've read something and it stated: Poverty is the worst kind of violence. 'NO MORE GOOD TIMES, NO MORE TIMES, TO HARD TO FIND, YOU'RE ALMOST BLIND -YOU COULD'NT SEE WHAT SPOT THAT THE TRAP WAS IN, Hey Bra...WHAT'S HAPPENING?'

And after the years and time is wasted, you're left with nothing. One thing remains certain if you're on the path to recovery, you're on your way to living, that's the main thing, living. Have a foundation of staying clean and sober. Prepare for the worst and the best will take care of itself. My foundations are God and myself, always keep a constant appraisal of loving yourself. And stay in constant prayer. People are not there for you when your crack and money is gone.

The continuation of Crack Spell

Marcy and Nancy were steady at their home group N.A meetings and was very active in their sobriety and doing quite well. Teresa was on her way to a probation hearing after serving six-years at a women's correctional facility. Teresa was sentenced to sixteen years, but because of her exceptional behavior she made parole. Teresa stepped out of her cell dressed in the orange jumpsuit, the guards shackled her up, and then they took a slow walk to the parole boardroom where her hearing was held.

Already seated in the office were the Warden, and a few power heads who governed the entire state penal institutions. Teresa took a seat as the Warden and the others looked over her file. There was a pause in the room, and then one of the authorities asks Teresa.

"If you were released back into society what would you do?"
"I would dedicate my life to God and my family and would get help for my drug addiction ma'am. I also would work and feed the homeless and hungry. I would basically do my part in making this a better society."
The panel was impressed with her answer.

"So I see that you have kids that are living with a relative and a potential job lined up." The Warden stated.

Yea, and I'm set up to attend parenting classes and NA meetings regular, I've learned so much in my time of being incarcerated that I know if I'm given the chance, I will be the best citizen that this society has to offer."

The panel just looked at each other with amazement. Then they huddled in conversation amongst themselves, silently speaking on her good behavior and her answers to the committee of what her activities would be in society. As Teresa sat quietly each one of the committee members faced her with a smile especially the lone female that sat on the panel that was dominated by men.

"Well Ms. Skipper, your file is very impressive and your behavior seems to be that of a model citizen," The Warden stated. He continued, "I believe whole heartily that if you are released early you would do the right thing, I really believe that Ms. Skipper. I'm just hoping that you don't make what I'm stating here to be untrue…am I making myself clear Ms. Skipper?"

"Crystal clear," Teresa stated as she sat quietly waiting for the call if whether she would be released from prison or not.

The panel conversed for a brief moment and made the decision to release her.

Meanwhile Trevor Skip Karp was having hard times of his own. Skip has served six years in prison already and was being tested every day by some inmate old or new. One occasion was when Skip was out on the Rec. yard and was just hanging out, when another inmate walked up to him and asked what was he in for. Skip's response was,

"I was at the wrong place at the wrong time."

The dude had psychological problems, and was quiet off. He told Skip that it was the wrong answer. Skip turned, and started to walk away when the dude took one hand and pulled Skip face to face with him and said,

"Nigga I said what you in for, and stop bullshitting with me!"

Skip response was urgent and swift; he took his closed and tight right fist and connected to the middle of the face of the stranger, as the two tussled on the Rec. grass other inmates were gathered around the fight urging them on. Soon the guards came out, and the stranger took a medal shank and stuck Skip numerous of times in his side, Legs and neck-then a friend of the stranger took a sock that had two combination locks in it and knocked Skip's right eye out. The guards broke up the fight and alerted the tower that they would need the paramedics on the scene. The guards soon had Skip and the inmate in the medical part of the prison getting put back together by the prison doctors.

Skip's right eye was totally lost and the doctors had to give him numerous stitches from the puncture wounds. The other guy had only small bruises. Skip on the other hand was lucky to be alive. He was on life support, but the doctors were saying that he would make it and pull through. One of Skip's associates in the prison notified his mother that he was in an accident and lost his right eye. His entire family was devastated especially his mother.

Meanwhile Teresa was being released from the women's prison, for good behavior after a six year stint. Her brother picked her up at the gate on a bright Saturday morning. Her older brother Cliff is a successful graphic artist at an Ad agency. He's a bachelor with no kids and he's the only relative that she has that's living, they remained close regardless of the circumstances. He was the one that took care of her kids, while she was locked down so for six.

Her two children ran quickly to her and they both jump in Teresa's arms for a warm embrace. They got into the car and had a cool relaxing drive to her brother's house, a nice four thousand sq. feet, and 5 bedroom, 2 bath home. Since he has no kids there is plenty of room.

Nancy has six years clean and is thinking about using again. Marcy is fine and has moved into nice home on the south side of town, she received a nice promotion at the hospital she's been working at since she graduated Junior college 18 months ago. She's still the same Marcy without the heavy drugs in her life. Judy is living well and is working as a secretary at a prominent local law firm; her two daughters are in high school and are near graduation. Nancy lives with this guy that works construction and they share a nice two bedroom apartment/home together.

It was Wednesday and Nancy had the day off from her job monitoring at risk youth, teen girls. It was about eleven-thirty am, and the temptation of taking a blast of crack was hitting her hard. She tried everything to get the thought of using off of her mind. She cleaned every room in the apartment from top to bottom, but the urge of hitting a nice piece of drop was heavy on her mind. She sat on the sofa and switched on the TV. She switched from channel to channel, the urge was still there, she picked up the phone and called Marcy, Marcy was at work and picked up the call on its first ring.

"Hello,"
"Yeah girl this is Nancy."
"What's up, you know Teresa was released from prison today." Marcy said.
"Oh really, where is she?"
"She's at her brother's house now. I'm going over there when I get off at about 5 this evening…you wanna go?"

"Yeah girl, I'll go, but it's something I really need to talk with you about...you got time?"

"Yeah, I just started this hour break, what's up?"

"I really got this urge to pick up. It started this morning when Dale left for work, of course I have the day off, and I've tried everything to get using off of my mind."

"Nancy whatever you do don't pick up, I'm going to tell Betty to call you. She runs the meetings locally and has twenty years clean. Whatever you do don't do it until you talk with Betty. To be real with you I've had urges and temptations come to my mind, but I realized that my using that shit won't cause me anything but trouble and pure hell. If I take a hit I'll ride that wave for one week, two weeks, maybe a month, but that shit will be all that I'll concentrate on. If I smoke that shit it's going to take away my pride, my Job, food...shit my entire life, that's why I stay away from it. I look at that shit like its fucking poison. That shit is going to destroy me, and then it's going to take away my life, whether it's death or prison. And I just can't give it to'em like that. Spending hundreds with a motherfucker and when I'm out of dope, I go back to see if I can get a dime from'em; guess what? Nothing. This motherfuckah can't even give me a ten dollar rock after I've spent 700 with the motherfuckah. That shit is poison, smoking that hard is slavery all over again."

"Yeah I feel you and all that, but I think," Marcy interrupted her in midspeech.

"That's what you're doing wrong, Nan you're trying to think this thing through, and you can't think crack addiction, you have to don't do crack. That should be your entire activity in life, to stay off of crack cocaine. Don't get high; Betty's going to call you. Be ready to go see Teresa when I come by there this evening. Remember don't pick up whatever you do, alright?"

"Got you, I'm feeling that shit." Nancy quickly said.

"Fuck feeling it, do that shit! Alright see you tonight, Marcy said."

They both hung up. Nancy's closest friend Faye had relapsed, but was still seeking help. Nancy would have to think swift and occupy herself: She changed the channels on the TV waiting on Betty's call. Thirty minutes has passed and still no call from this Betty.

Nancy decided to get up and look out of her blinds. She saw a young man on the corner she heard was holding some grade A base. Her mind was sold onto smoking, and when she had gotten to that point- the National Guard couldn't keep her from igniting that stem packed with crack. Nancy went to the bedroom and put on some shorts, sneakers and a top. She had just gotten paid a day before, so she had some two-hundred dollars left after paying half the rent and buying groceries. She grabbed two twenty dollar bills and a ten and headed out of the house, down three steps and onto the sidewalk and coolly walked down to the corner where the young man was waiting for customers.

"You holding?" Nancy asked.

"What you want, you aint Vice or the police or some shit like that is you?" The dealer questioned.

"Nah you've been seeing me, I live right there, she pointed to the house, man I want five dimes," she quickly said.

"Here you go, I got Twenties, I'll give you three for the fifty."

He put three fat twenty dollar pieces of crack into her hand; she looked at the dope and was so surprised of the size of the pieces that her vagina juiced up immediately.

"This aint no whab is it?"

"That there is straight butter. If it aint, come see me...alright?"

She handed him the fifty in cash and went back to the house. She hurried in the doorway and locked the door behind her. She sat on the sofa and remembered she had a glass Pyrex stem in one of her tote bags that she never threw away.

She kept it because it reminded of the very thing that took her down the road of poverty and shame, and she would look at the stem every now and then. She got up and went to the room to retrieve the stem. She then walked casually back to the livingroom and sat on the sofa. She grabbed a fresh razor blade that was on the bottom level of the coffee table, then she placed the drugs on the glass table and sliced up one of the thick pieces and placed it on the stem. She heated up the crack and inhaled the smoke, a sense of great accomplishment had surrounded her total being, and she hadn't accomplished a damn thing.

That's how crack makes one feel as if they've done something great and haven't done anything. The figh dope had her at the center of her existence.

She then placed the stem and lighter on the carpet beside the end of the sofa where she sat, then got up and peeped out of the blinds, smoke still seeping out of her nostrils.

The crack was tension, grade A cooked cocaine. Then the phone ranged, it was Betty. Nancy stepped back from the blinds to look at the ID on the phone, and saw a Betty Luv. She knew it was the lady calling her about staying clean and not picking up, but she ignored it and stared at the phone until the answering machine picked up, a low sophisticated feminine voice echoed out of the phone.

"HELLO, THIS IS BETTY LUV, MARCY TOLD ME TO GIVE YOU A CALL. HEY LISTEN WHATEVER YOU DO DON'T PICK-UP, TAKE GOD WITH YOU THROUGHOUT YOUR DAY AND EVENING AND REPLACE THAT BAD HABIT OF THOUGHT WITH SOMETHING GOOD, HOPE TO SPEAK WITH YOU SOON.

Nancy just stared at the answering machine for seemed like minutes, then she slowly moved back over to the couch where she mounted a bigger piece of the crack rock, she inhaled deep and held the smoke in and slowly exhaled it out of her nose. She suddenly thought that she had a live in boyfriend, and he could walk through the door at anytime. So she gathered all of the crack and paraphernalia and walked to the back room to hide it in her Tote bag.

Time had passed and she knew her boyfriend would be getting off of work soon, so she went to the front of the apartment dranked two shots of Hennessy and got in the shower. She dried off and then put on her panties, bra and a mini robe, and then laid on the bed and watched a court show, until she heard a key in the front door and it was her boyfriend. Nancy was cool from the Hennessy and when he made it to the back room she was seductively waiting for him.

Dale is a nice upwardly mobile man that has worked for the same construction company for six years and was a supervisor of a foundation crew. He never drank hard liquor; he'd have a beer or two but only on the weekends. He opened the door to the bedroom and there she was sprawled out on the bed looking as tasty as she's ever looked. They greeted each other and she quickly told him to shower and that she had something for him when he got out of the shower.

"And what's that?" Dale asked.

Nancy pointed to her pussy, which was visible through her see-through panties, then her mouth. He turned and quickly got into the shower. While he was in the shower she went into the tote bag and got out the crack, stem and lighter. She then placed them under one of the pillows and waited for him. He dried off quickly, and walked into the bedroom naked. Nancy gestured with one finger for him to come over as she sat on the edge of the bed. Dale walked over to her with a semi-erection. Nancy applied her best oral technique until she had his mind in the palm of her hand. He would do or try whatever now, because he loved Nancy. He knew of her past history with drugs, but never in his wildest dreams would he have thought that she would approach him about using crack cocaine.

"Baby you know I love you right?" Nancy asked.
"I guess. I hope so?" Dale responded.

"But first baby I need for you to go to the kitchen and get that bottle of cognac that's sitting on the counter, she continued, tonight I'm going to soak you down nice, you've been working hard baby and I just want to please you tonight okay."

Dale went to the kitchen and got the cognac and two glasses with ice in them, and headed back to the room. Before he put the drinks on the night stand they both took gulps of the liquor. Dale put the drinks on the stand, and Nancy quickly said,

"Baby taste me." Nancy opened up her thighs as Dale began to orally stimulate her. Her juices covered his face when she pulled the stem from under the pillow, which already had a block of crack melted in it. She struck the lighter and slowly inhaled the smoke and held it in. Dale heard the crackle of the flame making contact with the stem but paid it no attention. As Nancy exhaled the smoke, Dale could smell the potency of cocaine in the air, as Dale pressed up on his elbows to see what was going on, Nancy paused for about fifteen seconds and then spoke.

"I need for you to smoke this with me baby."

Dale didn't say a word, but watched as Nancy put another piece of crack on the stem. She held the stem to his mouth and flicked the lighter, as he inhaled, a stream of cocaine smoke flowed through the glass stem. He pulled away from the stem, as she told him to hold the smoke in for a second then exhale out of his nostrils. As he did that, Nancy grabbed his penis, and started sucking. He closed his eyes as Nancy slurped and salivated on his penis while the cocaine acted as a seductive aid in the matter.

Trevor 'Skip' Karp was healing well after weeks of the life threatening incident he was involved in. Mainly because of his enrollment in the Life Lessons course, given by the State to inmates. He was attending these classes six times a week, Tuesdays, Wednesdays, and Fridays. One hour each day after breakfast and two hours after dinner at night. The classes were helping him out allot, and after a week of taking the classes, he'd wish he had attended something like this when he was free on the outside. The core of the course was teaching Independence, Responsibility and Discipline. The course matures the man, and upon completion, he's able to automatically make right decisions. Trevor also attended a drug rehab and prevention from illegal narcotics course.

All the while, Nancy was heavily influencing Dale into becoming fully addicted to hell on earth (crack-cocaine).

"C'mon baby, eat my pussy while I take a hit."

Dale just looked at her grabbed her thighs, spreaded them apart and ate her out desperately.

"Oh, uhh... ooh shit," were Nancy's reactions to the oral onslaught she was receiving. She already had a piece of crack melted on the stem, as she pulled slowly while she was being eaten out. Beautiful was what she was feeling as she lightly flung the stem and the lighter to the floor in opposite directions. She then put her head back letting the smoke seep slowly out of her nose.

By this time it was 5 o'clock and Marcy was getting off of work. Her plans were to pick Nancy up, so that they both could go over to see their mutual friend Teresa, who had just been released from prison. Marcy dialed Nancy's number; there was no answer, so she decided to head over to Nancy's house. After about 20 minutes, Marcy was pulling up in front of her house. She walked to the door and knocked; no answer. She then walked around to the backroom window, where she saw Nancy and Dale igniting their glass stem.

"Nancy!" Marcy shouted.

Dale was shocked to see someone at his back window. Nancy scrambled to the window and told Marcy to meet her to the front door. Dale stayed in the back room while Nancy went to the front of the house wrapped in her robe. Nancy opens the door as Marcy comes in; Nancy sits on her sofa and poured herself a drink.

"You stuck on that shit, aint you?" She continued. Out of all that shit we've been through fucking with that and you went back to smoking? You know Betty called you earlier!" Marcy exclaimed.

They both took seats in the living room Nancy looked around the room feeling dejected and defeated and responded saying,

"I just couldn't help it, I tried everything in my power to avoid taking that first hit. I really tried.

"Girl you aint stupid. Do you remember when you almost got murdered from fucking with this shit, six years ago? Nancy you're my girl and I swear I'll kill a dead brick over you, and I'm busting ass if anybody fucks with you the wrong way, but are you going to live your life or are you going to let crack smoke live it for you. Put on your clothes…we're going to see Teresa, I don't care if you want another hit or not. You got 5 minutes."

Nancy knew Marcy was prone to fighting, so she didn't hesitate on getting ready to ride. She put on her a jump suite and sneakers, and they headed out.

Dale meanwhile was still in the back room, smoking the remains of the crack that was on the bedside table. He was running out of crack and was down to his last nickel piece of dope. He knew he needed more, so he got up and put on the same work clothes and boots that he had worked in that day, took a hundred dollars out of his wallet, slipped it into his pocket and went to the bedside table to smoke the last piece.

He inhaled the cocaine smoothly and took a drink of liquor, then headed out of the house. He walked to the corner and saw no 300 dollar bomb peddlers out trying to serve dimes and twenties, so he crossed the street over to the apartments. He ventured into the courtyard where he saw a beautiful Puerto Rican woman that looked to be about 5-4 a hundred and eighty pounds. Her name was 'Sugar' and she was fiending for some dope, but she was cool. Dale walked over to her standing at stair entrance of one of the apartment buildings.

"You know where I can cop some hard?"

"There is a dude on the third floor of this building named Die-Boy, he got jugglers of butter, just shoot me a dime."

"I'll shoot you more than that, I appreciate it." Dale stated.

Sugar waited on the front steps of the apartment, while Dale went up the stairs in anticipation of seeing his old hood friend, because Dale and Die grew up in the same neighborhood together. He got to the third floor and knocked on the door where he heard Chef Raekwon on a record…'BUT LATE NIGHT CANDLELIGHT FIEND WIT A CRACK PIPE, I GUESS IT'S ALLRIGHT FEELING HIGHER THAN AN AIRPLANE RIGHT, WORD YO, I'D RATHER TAKE THIS MONEY THEN BLOW and some potent Ganja smoke that permeated the hallway.

Dale knocked on the door.

Die opened the door.

"Boy what's up, thought you'd be running somebody's company by now." Replied Die as he continued on. "You see what I'm doing…what in the fuck happen man?"

"I got hurt in college, plus the lil scholarship I had… I didn't take full advantage of it, and I didn't play hard enough ball while I was out there." Responded Dale.

"Yo baby," Die said to his girlfriend, he continued.

"Hey baby this nigga suppose to be in the N.B.A. or playing Quarterback for one of those teams on Sunday". Die's girlfriend just smiled.

"Yeah man, so what's up CUZ?" Die asked.

"Man I need about a hundred dollars worth of that thang."

"What you talking bout some weed?"

"Nah, some hard."

"Ah, Dale you aint smoking is you my nigga?"

"Nah, I'm getting this for somebody else."

"I got you, hold up," Die said, he continued. "Baby go get that fresh package from the back and bring it here."

She went to the back to get the zip lock bag full of slabs and cookies of crack-cocaine her and Die had just cooked up.

"I aint gonna get into your business." Die-Boy said, as he went into the plastic bag, pulled out a slab that was worth about $200, and placed it on the table and Dale gave him the hundred dollar bill. Dale asked Die, if he had something to put the crack in.

"Baby, get him one of those baggies out of the cabinet." Dale put the dope inside of the baggy so that it wouldn't melt, the crack was freshly cooked.

"Yo man put this in a dry cool area, because I just took it out of the pot. Don't let it sit in this plastic baggy long either, or you'll have a cocaine milk shake. But yo man, you know where I'm at, come and see me," Die said.

"You got a number?" Dale asked.

"Nah man, I don't put myself out there like that, just come and see me. If I'm not here then she'll be here. Cool?"

"Cool."

They shook hands, and Dale stepped out of the apartment. As he got to the bottom of the stairs- Sugar was out waiting, she saw Dale and asked.

"You Straight?"

"Yeah," as he showed her the slab in the baggy.

"Yo man, break me a piece of that shit," she asked.

"Nah, come with me to my house." As he palmed squeezed the inside of Sugar's ass cheeks.

He started walking and she was directly beside him. When they got to the house they headed to the back room. No words were said. Sugar pulled her stem out of her bra as Dale mounted up a piece on his stem. He chopped her off a chunky piece of dope. Sugar grabbed the lighter that was on the bedside table and ignited her pipe, after she inhaled the cocaine; she put the stem on the bedside table and pulled down the tight spandex pants that she had on and revealed a red thong underneath, and the smoothest ass, hips and thighs Dale has seen in years.

It was about 7:10pm and Trevor Karp and his cell mate Macklin, a brother that is doing 40 years, and is on his 15th year. Macklin is a brother that is part of the Nation of Islam inside of the prison. His organization is real effective, and it teaches prisoners how to cope with prison life. He and Karp were just sitting in their cell talking.

"Yeah out there these butter soft Niggas be on some Bogie…some trying to be gangsta hard shit, until they get their ass up in here. Then they turn into bitches," snapped Trevor.

"Yeah they think being incarcerated is some ole sweet shit. I have to tell'em, nigga this is a whole new world in itself. Where you do what another nigga want you to do, or fight to the death nigga, because that's what it's about in here.

" Macklin continued on,

"I remember about my 4th year of being locked up they brought in a fresh bus load of them Gits, I was working in intake and this one lil nigga started poppin shit, talking about what he'll do to a nigga if they fuck with him and all that. Karp, that nigga said he'll kill this and kill that, I grabbed him and slammed him on that hard ass concrete floor and said you aint gonna kill nothing but a nigga nature."

Trevor laughed and told his cell mate,

"Man I got the new issue of "Big Black Butt' and 'Big Butt'. I need some release. I'm fixing to step into that stall and fuck the shit out of one these thick ass bitches in these magazines and she won't even know it."

"Knock yourself out brother, but tomorrow I need for you to sit in one of our sessions. The teachings and knowledge is butter, I know you'll find it very uplifting."

"Macklin I'm there just let me know the time."

"It's when everybody goes to Rec,"

"I'll be there."

M arcy and Nancy were pulling up to Teresa's brother's Split-Level 5 bedroom 2 bath home. Marcy gave Nancy a little talk before they got out of the car.

"Girl you know I'll always be there for you and I want you to be there for me, but I'm going to tell you… you've got one more time to pick up and use and I'm beating your ass."

Nancy was about to respond and Marcy viciously interrupted,

"I don't want to hear nothing, and I want tell Teresa about your lil shortcomings, let's just visit and chill, Alright." Nancy nodded yes, and got out of the car. They walked up the walkway and rang the doorbell. Teresa's brother was away and her two kids were playing in their new room upstairs. Teresa came to the door, looked out of the peephole, saw who it was and immediately opened the door.

With immense excitement Marcy and Nancy stepped into the open arms of Teresa. Marcy was very happy and so was Teresa, along with Nancy who was coming down off of that powerful geek, but was happy to see Teresa.

"Ya'll have a seat, I got some juice so what's up," as she opened the door of the refrigerator to get orange and apple juice.

"Yeah girl, what's up with you, you're alright?" Marcy asked.

"Yeah it was hard, but I just thought about my children and my brother and that got me through each day."

"Girl, you've gotten fat," Marcy commented.

"Yeah, that's what laying off of that shit and eating everyday will do for you. Oh, and I can't forget prayer, because without him I wouldn't have made it. God gets all the glory for everything. They just sat back and talked as the kids came down the stairs.

"Hey, Auntie Marcy and Nancy," they both said in synchronicity.

The kids felt great about having their mother home with them. For six years they've asked their uncle, "When are those people going to let our mommy come home." Nancy was coming down rapidly, and asked about Judy; the young lady who Nancy introduced the drug to.

"She wrote me once. She was sort of pissed at me for almost getting her 8 years." Teresa laughed as she continued to speak, "I've just been trying to stay cool through this whole thing, I wrote her back, but never received another letter, after that I concentrated on just doing that time, my kids, my brother and you two since ya'll were the only ones coming to visit me." Teresa gave a slight smile and said what I really wouldn't mind having right now… some boiled crabs, potatoes corn, crawfish, ya'll know." Marcy didn't hesitate.

"There is a 24 hour fresh seafood market that's on the south side, I think I got enough for three dozen," Marcy stated.

"Don't worry my brother left me one of his Visas," Teresa stated.

"Nah, I'm not having that, girl this is all on me -you relax, you just did six years lockdown. We just want you to concentrate on loving you and your kids, understand, and I'm going to make sure you do that first one alright?" Teresa had no reply, but smiled and stretched her arms out as if she was yawning.

"Hey ya'll go put on your shoes because we're leaving in 5 minutes," Teresa said to the kids.

"Yes ma'am." The kids went upstairs to put on shoes as Teresa stood up showing her banging figure.

"Damn girl, if I was a man, you'll be mines tonight, you thick as hell, Nancy stated finally coming down off of her geek.

"Ya'll think so?" Teresa asked.

"Hell yeah, as they all headed out of the front door, and got into Marcy's black 4 door, 2008 Audi 5000 coupe.

"I'm hoping that there is somebody descent out there. After doing all of that time I'm ready, but not that ready …ya'll have to excuse me, but after I was told that I know longer carried the virus I really wouldn't care if I have a partner or not…shit I'm just happy as hell I don't have that Ninja." Teresa said seriously.

"Yeah, it's not hard to find a good brother out here…you know a nigga that paid attention when he was growing up. Ya'll know what I'm talking about, he saw a relative go to prison so he's not incarcerated, he saw a kinfolk abuse drugs and became a high school dropout so he went to college and received his degree. I need a sharp ass nigga like that. You know a motherfuckah whose criminal record is as clean as Clorox. And they are out here! Marcy exclaimed as she started the car to make the trip to the seafood market. Then out of the blue Nancy stated.

" I think I got a good guy", with a little authority in her voice, now that she had fully come down off of her high. She continued. "He's alright, he pays bills, buys food, a very responsible dude, you know what I'm saying."

Marcy gave Nancy an agitated look in her rearview mirror. Since Nancy was referring to the guy who Marcy caught her smoking crack with earlier. It had started to slightly rain, and a car dotted out in front of them and she had the right of way. She honked her horn.
"Damn these are some non-driving mother-fuckers around here. Oh, excuse my language kids." The kids just smiled as they were sitting in the backseat with Nancy.
Then Teresa spoke sitting in the passenger seat.
"I'm saying that I just got out and I'm going to make the most of my life this time. I'm not letting anything or no one stop me from living the life I need and want for myself." She continued.
"I've learned so much while I was locked up. I easily could've been like some of those other girls running in cliques and packs, but I chose to roll Dolo…, because I had love ones on the outs, you know when ya'll would leave me from the visit, I'd say to myself…I got to get out of here."

They had finally reached the seafood market. They parked and walked in.

Teresa kept speaking as they look over the different selections of fresh fish that was on ice in the display case, and live blue clue crab that were in 3'by 3' wooden crates according to size, jumbo, large and medium.

"Yeah, the only scar that I have from being locked up is not being with my children day and night that's basically it. I know I'm not going to relapse because I have a plan for my success. My first plan is to stay away from crack and people who smoke crack...I wouldn't care who it is. My friends and associates are those trying to stay clean.

Uncle 'Scrap' was an old player in the city. Everybody called him 'Scrap' because in the late 60's and all of the 70's he was popular player and pimp. He use to always have a knot of cash, was tops in fashion, (his dress game was immaculate) and he always drove the latest cars. He ran women (pimped them) sold drugs until he got caught up into using his own grade A heroin that he supplied to every section of the city. 'Scrap' also had businesses, to disguise his illegal drug endeavors.

Die-Boy, Dale and all of the major players of today looked up to 'Scrap', especially Trevor 'Skip' Karp. All of the young crack dealers of today knew of' Scrap's' legend, so they respected him a great deal, even though they knew that he loved to smoke crack. If 'Scrap' wouldn't have gotten caught up in the hell-bound intoxicating pleasures of abusing heroin and crack, he would be financially set for life and wouldn't be homeless or struggling like the average derelict on the street.

He maintained his residence at different crack houses and missions around the city. He kept a 'Go' cell phone on him that Trevor had purchased for him before Karp became incarcerated.

A young brother that was a casual smoker was getting high at Dora's, one of Scrap's old girlfriends from the 70's.

"Nigga what you said your name was again?"

"Bowler Jack." Jaquel stated, as he handed 'Scrap' another piece of dope to smoke.

Scrap mounted the piece, held the stem up and ignited the pipe. He pulled off of the stem and held it up in the air as if he had some country's flag in his hand and watched the cocaine oil slowly make its way down the glass stem. He blew the smoke out and his teeth clinched tightly together.

"See that's it, yeah that's it right there boy…Man, you an alright old nigga." He said to Bowler Jack smacking his lips as he passed Dora the stem so she could hit her piece.

Big Dora was one of 'Scrap's old girl friends who ran one of the cleanest crack houses in that section of the city. Smokers use to love to come to Dora's and smoke, because they could smoke their dope in peace, and not get fucked with. Dora kept a sawed off pump 12 gauge rifle by her side when she had guest in. If anyone violated a person who has paid Dora to use her house, they'd get the wrath and it wasn't anything nice. So everyone always acted appropriate in Dora's crack den. Bowler Jack walked into Dora's house about 6:30 that evening and he and 'Scrap' hit it off immediately.

Bowler Jack is employed with United Stated Postal Service and it seems that every week after he's paid his bills he would smoke crack with money that he had leftover. He gave Dora 3 dime pieces, and 30 dollars cash for using her house, up until 11pm.

Dora's house is not the typical of the everyday crack den where the electricity is usually off and the toilet doesn't work and all you'll smell is backup waste throughout the house. Her place was clean; Dora always prided herself in having a clean home with lights, water and groceries. She works in the bakery department in one of the nicest grocery stores in the city; she's been there for twenty years. Dora would be classified as a functional smoker, not a crack head; there is a difference once again. The functional smoker dose not spend their every waking moment trying to get a hit of crack, as would a crack head. A functional smoker works and pays bills like a normal person; they'd just get high when the main crust of their business is taken care of. A Crack Head on the other hand is totally different, they'd rob steal, post up on corners selling whatever to get a blast of dope. Will not bathe work or eat, just smoke stem.

'Scrap' pulled Dora aside and mentioned that he was not letting Bowler Jack out of his sight, 'Scrap' didn't want the young man to be taken advantage of, which would've happen if he was at a different smokehouse other than Dora's.

Bowler Jack had been buying crack for Dora and 'Scrap' all night. And since he was green and didn't know the games that crack smokers run, 'Scrap' wanted to keep him there with them. 'Scrap' let Dora know that he was going up the street to get one of the best tricks in the city, a young lady that everybody called 'Off the Chain' because of her 6in. tongue and was so fine. Chain had a small waste and a 65 in. ass, and the prettiest breast any eyes had ever seen. She is a young lady that is 24 years of age.

She was raised in the neighboring county, came to the city when her mother and dad had died. Chain was raised as an only child in a moderately middle class home.

Her parents left her the 24 hundred sq. ft., 3bed 2 bath, 120,000 dollar home when they died. She resided at that home for about 4 months until she sold it for 20 thousand dollars to an up and coming lawyer. She sold the house so that she'll have the money to smoke crack. When she found herself homeless and hungry she moved to the city. She started out stripping at a popular Gentlemen's club, until she couldn't perform properly any longer, because she was so preoccupied with smoking crack. She eventually landed on the streets, where she started tricking for crack and food.

'Scrap' knew Bowler Jack wanted to enjoy himself, so he whispered to Dora that he was going up the street and for her to not let Bowler Jack leave for anything. Ten minutes had past and 'Scrap walks in the door with 'Off the Chain'. Dora introduced herself and let 'Scrap' know that the young man's time was running out and that he'd have either give up some more money or dope if he wanted to continue to get high in her house, 'Scrap' nodded in agreeance 'Scrap' walked inside of the room where Bowler Jack was slumped over in a chair in the bedroom.

"Straighten yourself up nigga, this girl want to throw some this good pussy on you."

'Off the Chain, whose real name is Karin, stood there in some tight blue booty shorts, a blue halter top that hugged her 42 in. DD breast perfect, and a pair of casual brown sandals. 'Scrap' put down 3 dime blocks he'd copped from Die Boy, on his way to getting 'Off the Chain'. 'Bowler Jack' just stared at 'Off the Chain's womanhood, he couldn't believe that a woman was that well proportioned.

"Get yourself in the right perspective nigga and fuck some of this sweet pussy, and feed her some of that dope there I just got from up the street - Baby take care of this nigga… you hear me?" Scrap said.

'Off the Chain' just nodded yes, as 'Scrap' took a power blast, while standing in the door-way.

"Damn that nigger be having some figh ass shit," as he exhale the smoke and closed the door on Chain and Bowler Jack. Scrap then went into the living room and gave Dora the stem

"Now c'mon on and get on this dick." Scrap told Dora.

'Off the Chain' stood in front of him as he handed her the stem with a dime on it. She sat beside him on the bed, put the stem to his mouth and lit it.

"Inhale slow now pull hard," she said to him. As he pulled away from the stem and laid back on the bed. Chain unzipped the jeans he had on, and started giving him the sloppiest head ever, she deep throated him and took his sack into her mouth at the same time for about 3 minutes straight, until she made him cum in her throat, between the dope and the oral pleasure he had received. He was in heaven.

"Oh damn baby!" Was all that Bowler Jack could say, since he was in a great state of gratification.

"Here now you can smoke." Bowler Jack said to 'Off the Chain'.

She paused and stared at him for a second and said, "Nah nigga I want to fuck, I haven't been fuck good in a long time, you think you can handle that, I got some KY Jelly, we'll talk about smoking when you do this." She got on all fours and parted her ass cheeks for him, as he buried his tongue between her cheeks.

"Yeah that's cool, now lock that door and cut the lights out and light that candle that's on that bedside table, and if anybody comes to it just ignore them motherfuckahs." Jack did as she said, got back into the bed lubed himself up then he squirted a glob of the Jelly between Chain's cheeks, as she parted them with her hands. He inserted and tried to rush-

"Hold up, slow down nigga, this aint no pussy, you going in me to fast, work it slow," she said to him with a tone of womanly submission to her voice.

"Ah, yeah that's it…that feels good," as Bowler Jack worked till the hilt was buried in her. He started to thrust back and forth but not too many times, her ass was tight and juicy and drew an orgasm from Jack rather quickly as he released into her.

"Oh damn," he cried out rather loud.

There was a sudden knock on the door.

"'Nigger you alright in there," Scrap ask from the other side, as he tried to turn the knob but it was locked. Chain stretched out on the bed and gestured to him to keep silent.

"Yeah man, he's alright, I got him!" Chain cooly shouted to Scrap.

"Yo, tell'em that we aint got nothing to smoke, I'll go get a fifty piece from that dude. I need for him to slide fifty dollars under the door," Scrap stated back.

"Hold on." She said. "He'll be out in a couple of minutes," Chain said. As they both lay in the dem lit room naked and sweaty.

"You did alright, now I'm gonna put you up on game… man they trying to juice you and you don't even know it or probably know it and don't give a damn. Them bitches been smoking on you all night haven't they?"

"Yeah."

"Bout how much loot you got left?" She asked him.

"Bout six yards."

"Nigga they aint gone do nothing but smoke you up, bleed the hell out of you, then throw your ass out when you don't have no money and dope to give'em. You're their sucker, but fuck that, these niggas in this crack game don't play fair, get broke and can't get any more dope to give'em and see what happens. See the way they treat you then… you know what I'm saying.

Where do you work?"

"At the Post Office, been there for 3 years. I'm off tomorrow, but I have to go in the following day, I have a roommate and he doesn't know that I get down."

"Alright then, we're getting a motel room over where I we can flip at least 300 into 600 and you'll make a profit and still have something to smoke. See I'm about real…I don't do dumb shit, and you're going to take your ass to work when it's time to go to work. I'm trying to have something my nigga. Tell those two in there, you're going to run to your place and I'm riding with you. You really don't owe them an explanation for shit. Man I'm for your benefit if you're stupid enough to hang around and get bled by two dumb mother-fuckers then you do that, I'm telling you what's up, get unstuck my nigga let's get some liquor, some powder and chill." She adamantly stated.

Chain had gathered all of the remaining pieces of crack and crumbs in a little make-up container and stuffed it back into her purse. They both put back on their close and were ready to make an exit.

"Alright my nigga, when I hit this piece of dope - open the door and we're heading straight out of here, you got your keys baby?" She asked.

That word baby coming from her brought a smile to him inwardly since it was coming from Chain whom he'd admired already. She was attractive, strong and intelligent, someone that if she wasn't smoking could move some things. She would be the model woman if she ever got delivered from crack addiction. Chain put the flame to the stem and chiefed the dope professionally.

Jack opened the door as she exhaled the smoke and both made a B-Line for the front door without saying a word.

"What's happening Cuz?" Scrap asked Bowler Jack.

"Man I got to go handle some things at my home, I'll be back shortly."

Knowing in his mind that he'll never come near them again, or at least anytime soon. Jack continued.

"I have to go to my house, my roommate needs something, y'all be cool."

As Bowler Jack and Chain drove off all 'Scrap' could do was look out of the window.

"It was that bitch you brought up in here that made him leave," Dora said to Scrap rather angrily.

Scrap couldn't say or do anything, instead he agreed silently. All the while, Bowler Jack and Chain were headed towards taken care of their business on the other side of town.

Bowler Jack cut the AC on low and turn the volume up a little, 'I'M THE R, THE A, TO THE K.I.M., IF I WASN'T THEN WHY WOULD I SAY I AM,' pulsated throughout the truck from the Bose system.

"Damn man this is a nice truck."

"Thanks."

The vehicle was a 2007 Cadillac Escalade.

"So how'd you get the name Bowler Jack?" She asked.

"When I was about six, my mama took me to get a haircut for the first day of school, when I got back to the neighborhood all of my partners were calling me 'Ball Head' plus my name is Jacquel so you figure it out. Then I went and got another haircut about four months later, and they were hollering that it looked as if the barber had put a bowl on my head and cut around it. So they started calling me 'Soup Bowl,' then one of my uncles dropped the soup and just started calling me Bowler Jack, then the name stuck and it spread."

Marcy, Nancy, Teresa and the kids were in Teresa's brother's kitchen with a pot of live crabs in seasoned boiling water on the stove. They had the works in the crab pot; sausage, potatoes, oysters and corn on the cob.

"Marcy I really appreciate you being there for me girl, I really mean that," Teresa sincerely said.

"Don't even sweat that. I know you've been through a hard time, and I feel we all need each other in a good way from time to time constantly, but it's sad that we don't even know that, instead we cut, steal and rob each other for each other's soul," Marcy declared.

"Nancy smiled and Teresa was impressed and added on- "In prison I've seen young girls come in with no one in there corner, no letters, visits or nothing so they hook up and befriend those who use and abuse them, they stay linked up with them because they just want somebody, Teresa exclaimed.

"That's sad," Nancy said, as she finally spoke. "That's like that girl down the street from Dale and I. That nigga curse her, take her check and buy dope with it and beat the shit out of her if she say a word."

"Now that's bondage, shiiit," Marcy stated. And she'd always have to take her kids down to the mission to get a bite to eat. She thinks that there's no one but that slabby ass nigga, Nancy said emphatically.

"Mother-fuckahs are going through that kind of shit daily in this world, linking up and staying linked up in relationships that mean them no damn good. I'll be damn if I stay for a minute. As soon as motherfucker show me that they don't appreciate my love and friendship I'm out, and that's my word to the Black Goddess on that shit... feel me?" Marcy strongly stated.

They all laughed and Teresa pulled out the baking pans so that each of them had one for their crabs. "A good true man is definitely hard to find, It's either the good man is with a dumb ass bitch or the good woman is with a clown ass nigga…and I'm not discriminating when I say that, they can bury that skin color shit somewhere else. But it's definitely a blessing when two good people hook up and it happens quite often, you'll be surprised." Nancy said while taking a bite of her corn.

"Most niggas out here are either in jail or on their way to jail, faggots or unemployed, homeless smoking crack or some shit," Marcy said as she sucked the juice out the back of a female crab she'd-just opened.

"I think I have somebody good," remarked Nancy as Marcy gave her sordid stare, since Nancy was referring to the guy that Marcy saw her smoking crack with earlier. She continued,

"He pays bills, buys groceries for the house, you know take care of business, I think I need to call him to see if he's ok,"

"Yeah, you can use that phone that's hanging on the wall right there," said Teresa as she busted open a male crab and sucked up an oyster.

"Damn Marcy you seasoned these," Teresa said.

"Yeah she put her foot in these," Nancy remarked as she dialed her line.

The phone just ranged and after its sixth rang the answering machine came on. "HEY PICK UP THE PHONE, IF YOU'RE THERE, LOVE YOU." Dale was sexing Sugar and they were heavily into it, he ignored the phone call. They were both smoking crack and Dale was giving Sugar oral sex. All of the lights were off in the house except for the lamp, which sat on the bedside table of the bedroom they were in. And since the crack was drop they didn't have to rush through it. After both of them were done from their sexual escapades they layed down in the bed and smoked while they watched a porno movie with the volume on low.

"He's not answering my calls."

"He's probably violating your bed," Marcy said strongly and seriously.

"Oh dayuuum," sounded Teresa as she laughed a little and said.

"Girl sit down and drink this strawberry smoothie I just made and let all of that go. What's happening with us is most important, I'm not caring what a motherfuckah does out here, and that's real. Always putting a motherfucker who we are fucking or in a relationship with equal or above ourselves, then when those motherfuckahs cheat on us; we wanna jump off a bridge, get a gun, bleach some clothes and all of that silly ass shit. Like my daddy always told me since I was a little girl, he'd say, "Any motherfuckah that's born out of a pussy is bound to fuck up. As it says in the Holy Scriptures, Trust no man." Nancy you're older than me girl that should be your mind set also," Teresa said. Nancy had a look of worry on her face, but her friends comforted her.

"Damn baby, I like this…this is a good movie, and. the dope is pineapple crush, butter know what I'm saying," Sugar stated. Dale paid her words no attention, and mounted up a block of crack and smoked it.

"You married or do you have a girl living with you?" Sugar asked.

"Nah, Dale said as he mounted up another slug and smoked it without pushing the stem for the back. He got up and went to the closet instead of responding and pulled out about 400 dollars from his coat pocket and brought it to the bed where Sugar was hitting a piece and looked over at the cash that was on the bed and grabbed Dale's penis and started to deep-throat the brother rather expertly.

"Uhh, oh shit baby, you a bitch...a fucking bitch!" Was his reaction to the oral expertise of Sugar. The smoking and the fellatio went on for about 50 straight minutes, and Sugar and Dale was about to run out of crack to smoke.

Marcy, Teresa and Nancy had spent all night enjoying each other's company over Seafood and strawberry smoothies. The kids were put to bed and Teresa's brother Cliff was at a lady friend's house, chilling.

"Damn, he isn't answering any of my calls."

"Well, we all know that strange activities bring about strange situations or vice versa," Marcy said.

Nancy just listened and didn't think about what was said. Instead the ladies indulge in an Orco based cheese cake for dessert.

D ale was in such a debilitative state to move and was terribly paranoid so he told Sugar to go and cop the dope from Die and come back, as he stated in a very ghosting and stuttering way.

"Yu, yu, yu you can go get us bout 200 worth fra, fra, from Da, Da, Die can't you?"

"Yeah, I'll go to his place and cop 200, but what I need for you to do nigga is wait here until I get back, you're too fucked up to do anything."

Sugar went to the dresser and squeezed into a pair of Nancy's panties and put on one of Nancy's sweat suites that was in the closet, the pink sweat suit fitted her tight, since she was two sizes larger than Nancy. Though the outfit was rather tight, it was clean and served its purpose. She placed one of the hundred dollar bills in the crotch of the panties she wore. Sugar knew Dale was out of it

"C'mon man and lock the door, I'll be back in a couple of minutes." Sugar stepped out of the house and Dale locked the door and walked into the living room area and found a half of a Newport laying in ashtrey and lit it. He stumbled back into the backroom and took a wire hanger that was in the closet stretched the tip of it out until it was straight and attempted to pushed the cocaine packed piece of brillo that was in the glass stem. The stem was so full of coke that he had to heat the stem so that the brillo would go to the other end.

He put heat to the stem and puffed. A full cloud of potent cocaine smoke came seeping out the sides of his mouth, he was comatose. Caviar was what he was smoking, cocaine caviar.

Sugar crossed the street and headed for the third floor of the apartment building where Die- Boy and his lady Sheena was smoking herb. 'YOU COULDN'T CATCH ME IN THE STREETS WITHOUT A TON OF REEFER, THAT'S LIKE MALCOLM X CATCHING THE JUNGLE FEVER' ~ blared out of Die's stereo system out into the hallway of the apartment. Sugar knocked on Die's door.

"Who is it?"
"This Sugar." He opened the door.
"Man I need ten blocks." She handed Die a hundred dollar bill.

"Sugar where'd you get all of this loot from?" Sugar has never come to him with that amount of money, ever. The most she'd ever come to spend was 20 dollars, and he's been dealing with her for 2 years.

"Baby go get twelve of them thangs out the back." Sheena, Die's old lady got up without any questions went to the back and put 12 crack bricks into a plastic baggy, brought it to the front and put it in Sugar's hand.

"You can sell them for quarters," Die told her.
"Hell yeah, I'll see y'all." Sugar had got so excited over the deal that she didn't want to mixed words.
"Thank you Die...nigga you aight, I'll see you girl." Sugar said to Sheena as Sheena closed the door behind her.

Sugar started down the stair case and stuffed the baggy of crack in the crotch of her panties where the other hundred dollar bill was. She walked down the flight of stairs into the courtyard; she looked around and there was no one there. She made a move to a room she occupied at this decrepit two story rooming house, about two blocks from Dale and Nancy's house and the apartment complex where she copped the crack at.

Sugar's room was on the first floor; she stepped to the front and unlocked the door to the house with one of the two keys she kept on a key bob. She locked the door behind her and headed straight for her room. It was sort of late so everyone was asleep or in their own room entertaining or smoking dope.

She stepped into her room, locked the door with the little hook latch which was a second lock on her door, she undressed and slipped into a robe and opened the only window in the room for ventilation, but kept the blinds closed. She put the crack on the bedside table then switched on T.V. which sat on an old stand she bought from the thrift store for $2.

Sugar is a certified crack head and had several guns or stems lying around in her room. With her beautiful features and youth she could do any constructive thing she wanted, but her game was stuck in a crack stem and her life exemplified the fruits she obtained from that activity.

She had closed all of the windows in the room she occupied, switched the TV on low and cut the lights off. She stripped down to her panties placed the baggy of crack and the hundred dollar bill on the TV stand. She broke a piece of one of the large dimes and melted it on the stem; she paused then flicked the lighter and took a blast of it. She then looked around and hit the mute on the TV and laid back and mounted another piece.

She hit it, laid the stem and lighter on the floor and pulled out a Dildo and started massaging her clitoris. After she brought herself to an orgasm, she laid back on the pillow and heard a sudden bump on the side of the house, she jumped up already heavily geeked and paranoid, she crept to the window and found it to be just a metal garden rake colliding against the house. She looked out of the window and decided to go back to Dale's house and get high; she figured there she'd be more comfortable and relaxed.

Sugar stepped from the window and put on the clean tight fitting panties and the pink jogging suit that Dale gave her to wear, along with the sneakers she wore.

She put the remainder of the crack inside of the pill bottle so that it wouldn't melt and the wrapped the stem in a clean cloth and secured it in her panties inside of the folds of her vagina.

Dale had left the house looking for Sugar. He knew she had 49 faked him. He knew she wasn't coming back. He put on his work clothes that he had on earlier, and left the house looking for Sugar. He took a fifty dollar bill with him. He approached the apartment complex where he had met Sugar earlier. He saw an old man standing in the courtyard under a lamppost, Dale walked over to the old man and asked if he, the old man had seen a Puerto Rican chick real pretty dressed in pink around the apartments lately.

"Oh, you talking bout Sugar." The old stranger said.

"Yeah, that's her, man I gave her some loot to cop some dope for me." Dale stated.

"Oh, that's where she got all of that dope from… you, ha, ha, man Sugar don't ever have money or dope. Yeah she was here earlier, she even gave me a dime and that's unlike her man."

"Do you know where she's at?" Dale asked.

"She headed towards that old rooming house where she rents a room at, that one on Harlow, it easy to find man, but if you got a blast for the old man, I'll take you there personally."

"Yeah, I can do that, look here, give me two minutes, and let me holler at my man."

Dale climbed the flight of stairs and knocked on Die Boy's door.

"Who is it, shouted Die-Boy, as he peeped though the peephole, and when he saw who it was he immediately opened the door.

Dale, because of the previous crack usage, was looking uneasy and fidgety so he didn't say a word. He didn't want Die to know that he was fucked up, but Die has been selling crack for years and can spot a smoker a mile away.

"Boy C'mon in, Die said.

"Oh man this is Sheena my baby, she sticks by me man. She watches out when those silly-ass niggas come in here trying to throw curve balls and shit…y'know what I'm saying."

"Yeah, I know what you're saying."

"So what's up Dale, you know what I do, the same thing I was doing when I was coming up in the hood, knocking niggas out and selling dope," Die stated.

"Man you seen this Puerto Rican girl, dressed in pink come by here." Dale asked.

"Baby he talking bout Sugar, Dale you smoking man, cause that's all she does."

"Nah, man, I just trick with that shit, you know what I'm saying." Dale said.

Die knew better and decided not to get into his business, but knew from his actions that he was smoking.

"Man she left here about 30 minutes ago, that must have been your money she had, because Sugar don't ever have a damn thing, she came through here and copped 12, I guess that was your loot she spent." Die told him.

Dale looked a bit stupid, as he was anxious to get out of there, and start his search for Sugar and get him another hit, because he was desperately fiending for a hit.

"Yo man, you think I can get five of them thangs from you?" Dale asked, while handing Die a fifty dollar bill.

"Sheena gone back there and get 5 of them fresh blocks back there, alright baby."

She went to the back and got the crack, then placed them in Dale's hand. Die recognized quickly that Dale was trying to get somewhere and get him a blast.

"Man I aint gonna hold you up, but I'll see ya my nigga, come through and holla at me."

"Alright, I'll do that." Dale said as he left the apartment and headed down the flight of stairs to meet up with the old man that can help him find Sugar.

"'Damn man it took you long enough," the stranger said.

"Man, what do they call you anyway?" Dale asked.

"Crow. Man fuck all that, give me a piece of that dope, so I can show you where that girl is that's got your money."

"Man, you can't hit that shit out here in the open like this!" Dale interjected.

"Alright nigga… then stand there and watch me. You wanna find that bitch that's got your money and dope, don't you?" Crow retorted.

"Yeah man." Dale answered quickly.

"Then chill out, ole nigga, and leave me the fuck alone... let me chief this dope right here and we can be on our way, alright." Crow told him.

Dale shook his head Yeah, in agreeance. Crow had an old broken stem in his pocket. Crow fired up the stem and took a long pull. As soon as he exhaled the smoke, sirens sounded along with floods lights from a squad car. Then one of the officer's demands thundered through the speakers on the squad car.

"Put ya hands in air and spread out on the ground slowly."

Both crow and Dale laid down spread eagle on the ground. The officers got out of the car and patted both of the guys down. Both of the officers knew Crow.

"Crow, didn't we just let you out of the county 2 weeks ago." stated one of the officers.

"Nigger suck a dick", Crow said to the officer.

"Yeah, but you going to the county, and I'm gonna make sure that they give you more time than that lil shit they're always giving you." The officer stated.

"Whatever nigga." Crow said to the officer, he continued. "Hey officer, would you do me a favor before we go?" Crow questioned.

"What?"

"Let me push that stem first."

The officers laughed, then shove Dale and Crow in the back of the squad car.

The police confiscated 4 rocks and some cash from Dale, and since Crow threw the stem in the bushes that he hit the dime on, they only got a nickel bag of weed off of Crow.

Crow and Dale were booked and put into lock-up.

On the other hand Sugar was on her way back to Dale's house, with the dope and money stuffed inside of her panties. Marcy was giving Nancy a drop off at the place that Nancy and Dale shared. It must've been about 12 or 1o'clock in the morning. Nancy turned the key to her front door and the ladies were in. Marcy took a seat on the couch, in the living room.

"Girl I'm tired and happy, tired from working all day at that hospital and happy that Teresa's out of prison." Marcy stated.

"Dale"!! Nancy clamored throughout the house in hopes that her man would be there. Nancy went to the front of the house.

"Girl, he's nowhere in here." Nancy expressed.

There was a sudden knock at the door, Marcy went to see who it was, and Nancy followed her. Marcy opened the door.

"Oh, I apologize, I may have the wrong house," Sugar expressed emphatically.

Nancy looked and aggressively moved Marcy to the side when she recognized that Sugar had on her pink sweat suit.

"Nah bitch, you got the right house." Nancy expressed urgently as she pushed Marcy to the side and went after her. Sugar attempted to run, but Nancy caught up with her. Nancy grabbed Sugar by her hair and started pummeling Sugar so brutally; you would have thought it was the U.S versus Al Qaida. Marcy stood back and didn't interject. Nancy smashed up Sugar so bad you would've thought she had assaulted Sugar with a night stick or some other rigid object.

Nancy pulled the bloodied sweat suit off of Sugar, who was now sprawled out on the grass with nothing on but her panties which was holding the dope and money. The dope and money were protruding out of her panties. Marcy rushed in to grab Nancy and started pulling her friend inside, they got to the steps and Nancy shouted.

"Bitch, don't ever come around this spot again, I'll demolish you Hoe!"

Marcy pushed her friend inside of the house and locked the door.

Sugar was nearly unconscious, but managed to get the drugs and money out of her panties and slung them across the street, and due to her condition and strength she wasn't able to throw them very far but she got them off of her. She manages to crawl over to this older lady's house that lives next to Nancy and knocked on the door. The lady saw Sugar's condition, called 911 and told them to send an ambulance. Sugar was broke-up and injured very badly.

The lady was trying to get information from Sugar, but Sugar couldn't respond to anything. She was totally incoherent, and when the cops and ambulance had arrived her condition had seemed to have gotten worse. So they put her on the gurney and rushed her to the nearest emergency room. The lady didn't know anything about the incident, so she couldn't give the officers any information. The police then went over to Nancy's house. Both Nancy and Marcy responded that they didn't know anything of the incident. The cops had to chalk it up it and kept the case open; they even gave Nancy and Marcy the card with the number to the Police Department on it, telling them to call if they ever find out anything. Marcy and Nancy were very calm when they were questioned by the police. Revealing nothing to the officers.

"Damn girl why you had to do it like that."

Nancy looked despondent. Marcy made sure that she was alright before she left. She told Nancy that she'll call her when she gets to the house.

Sugar was taken to the emergency room her wounds were pretty bad, but the doctors were mainly concerned about her brain. When she and Nancy were having the altercation her head hit a boulder that was lying in the yard. Sugar was checking in and out, the doctors would take care of her though and the lead Doctor let everyone know that she would be alright.

'Off the Chain' and Bowler Jack were secured in their hotel room, they had been smoking and sexing all night, after Chain rescued Bowler Jack the night before from 'Scrap' at Dora's crack house. Chain went to a girlfriend of hers who sold weight and they got a deal for $300, nearly $600 dollars worth of grade A crack. Chain had a towel around her, ready to get into the shower, while Bowler Jack just laid in the middle of the bed watching the news, and getting ready to mount up a piece of dope.

"Hold up man, we aint doing anymore smoking today, we got to handle business. Look here my girl sells powder. I'll get you some of that and you can lay back and chill while I go out on this strip and make this money. We have to be patient with this, we aint smoking nothing and you're taking your ass to work tomorrow, what time do you have to be there?"

"5 in the morning," answered Jack while putting the stem down with Crack smoke still flowing devilishly through the glass stem.

"What I told you, we have smoked lovely all night and still got dope to sell and I'll make all that back that we've spent. If you would've stayed round those two 'Tack Head' mother-fuckahs you'll be broke and they would've kicked you out of that house. Let's get this money man, let's make this shit happen!" Chain explained.

Jack just listened to her and fired up a Newport cigarette and sipped on some Hennessy that was in a plastic cup. She continued.

"When I get out of this shower I need to go to that clothing store up the street and get a pair of pants and a clean blouse, alright?"

"Alright."

Chain went in to take a shower. The shower was hot and satisfying, then she stepped her naked lovely body out of the shower wrapped herself up in a towel. She suddenly heard a crackling noise and rushed out of the bathroom. Bowler Jack had just put the hot stem on the bedside table and had smoke coming out of his nose and mouth, 'Chain', scolded him…

"Let me lay it down to you like this my nigga. Now I was raised nice with a loving mother the whole nine and it was my ignorance to incorporate streets and crack smoking into my life. If you're going to smoke today let me know and we can part ways. I want the chance to change my life and I want it with you since you have the resources to do it with; a good job, nice truck, etcetera. But if you're not going to do what I say, then we can part ways now. Man I've seen this shit take down the best, Lawyers, Doctors…when I first started smoking that's who I use to trick with, that caliber of people. They went down fast, lost homes, cars, and loving family members and careers, so I migrated to the ghetto, where niggas struggle to survive, and my livelihood and style has been down ever since. I'm on the come up now and I know for certain that crack cocaine will leave you with nothing." Chain spoke adamantly.

"Yeah, I'm going to stop smoking this shit, it's getting the best of me." Jack said.

"Man it's time to move, take me down to that store to get something clean to wear and I'll flip this dope." She said.

Chain and Jack got dressed; Chain divided the drugs up into quarter pieces and put it in a plastic ice baggy that was on the hotel room's dresser.

"Look here man, I'm going to say this one last time, do not let anyone up in this room, and think of reporting to work tomorrow at 5 am." Chain stated while bagging up the drugs and putting them into her purse.

Jack tucked in his white t-shirt which was now a little dirty into his jeans, fastened his belt and slid on the pair of leather Jamaican Wallaby Clarks. They headed out of the door and down the stairs to the truck. Jack unlocked the doors and they got in. When they walked inside to the clothing store Chain asked the attendant for a pair of jeans and a blouse, along with a pair of sandals to match.

The sales lady hooked Chain up with the outfit she wanted and led her to the dressing room to try it on. The jeans were tight and accentuated her voluptuous figure along with the blouse, and the sandals were comfortable. She let the attendant know that she was wearing the outfit out of the store and that Jack was paying for it. The sales lady put Chain's old clothing into a store bag and wrung the tags of the new clothing up, Jack paid the lady, and they left the store and headed back to the hotel.

"Man you look like you're still tweaking from that last blast you took." Jack said nothing but kept his eyes on the road. Instead he told her that she looked nice.

"So how does it feel to have a good woman at your side?" Chain asked vigorously.

"It feels great. That's if you really want to be my woman. You know I'm a Capricorn and I move fast. I have the tendency to wear my heart on my shoulders...don't break my heart." Jack said emphatically.

"I'll do my part; you just go to work and do your part. When I serve all of this dope we're going out, to the movies and a seafood restaurant. I haven't done that type of normal shit in so long, I probably wouldn't know how to act...I'm just bullshitting, but for real though... I really need to do that type of shit. And when we get back to the hotel I need for you to break my ass open tonight, so stay off the shit and get your rest, we got to make this shit happen and I know we can as long as you're not smoking that shit." Chain stated.

They arrived in the Hotel parking lot, Chain told Jack to take the bag up to the room and she needed to hit the strip immediately. She told him that when she's through flipping the dope, they'll go and re-up. Then close shop around six and go out, come back and fuck and get some rest for the next day.

"Damn, I'm with that." Jack responded. He already respected Chain's knowledge and cared for her as a mate, he's finally with someone he could trust, and she's stunningly beautiful, he almost couldn't believe that this was the same chick that 'Scrap' brought to him from off the block. She arrived on the strip where there were old men drinking and talking shit in front of a convenient store. Chain posted up across from the store at a Mercedes Benz car lot. Suddenly a thick beautiful white chick walks up to her and asked…

"Do you know where I can get some hard at around here?"
Chain looked at the lady, up and down, then asked…
"You aint the police are you?"

"No," responded the pretty woman, She continued, "I've got this trucker that's parked at that hotel over there," she pointed to the hotel where Chain was staying. The lady continued. "He's been on the road all night and he just wants me to fuck him and get him some good dope."
Chain studied the woman and an asked her how much she wanted.

"Well he gave me a hundred dollar bill, get me $75dollars worth and I'm pocketing the other twenty-five." The woman spoke.
"Yeah, that's the way you do it, Chain said to her. Go over there to that store that's across the street and wait for me in that alley, I'll be there, alright?"

"Alright," the lady said dodging the cars on the highway to get safely across the street. Chain went inside of her purse and got three healthy quarter pieces out of the plastic bag, then cross the highway herself, she spoke to the old men that were out in front of the store drinking, then took a B-line to the alleyway. She handed the woman the dope and the woman gave her the hundred dollar bill.

"I don't have any change, let's walk in the store and break that hundred." Chain said. They walked inside of the store and the lady knew that she'd have to buy something, if she wanted to get the big bill changed.

"Get him some of that Cisco, it's the closest thing to a strong drink that they have in here." Chain said. The lady went to the beer cooler and got a Cisco. The man behind the counter wrung her up and broke the bill. She and Chain walked out of the store and the lady slipped Chain 75 dollars. Chain and the lady separated. The lady smoothly walked across the highway with the alcohol and dope in hand and the rest of the change in her pocket.

All the while, Teresa was headed over to Nancy's house to pick her up for the N.A meeting. She arrived at Nancy's house about 1 o'clock. Teresa knocked on the door then turned the knob, the door was open and she let herself in.

"Nan, you in here?" Teresa shouted while standing in Nancy's living room.

"Yeah, have a seat in there, I'll be out." Nancy shouted.

A couple of minutes had elapsed before Nancy stepped into her living room with a black and brown wrap dress on, that fell to the knee, some ultra sheer flesh tone brown stockings and some black ankle strap open toe stilettos with diamonds running up the middle, with a gold medallion broche wrap closely around her neck.

"Damn girl, you're looking like you're trying to catch a dude instead of going to an N.A. meeting. You know that dude you got is not going to allow that," Teresa said.

"Yeah, if he's clean and sober and is going forward in life...we're headed to the right place for that, and if he's got his shit together. The next man got to have something. If he aint making no money, he should try to act like he's making some, then I might let a man like that into my world. And that dude I had... that's past tense. He's locked up now for being green as fuck. Thinking he could just come out here smoking dope on some brand new...know what I'm saying. So I'm looking... I'm totally available." Nancy sincerely stated.

They both stepped out of the house and got inside of the car. Teresa cranked up the car and they were headed out for the N A meeting. They both were silent until Nancy pulled down the visor and applied a heavy layer of lip gloss.

"Yeah he had some bitch in my house last night, when Marcy and I got to the house. That chick came looking for him, talking bout she had the wrong house and guess what? She had the nerve to have on one of my sweat suits. I beat that Hoe down. Anyway forget about all of that, how was it doing that time?" Nancy asked as Teresa was trying not to travel over the speed limit.

"I read books and masturbated allot. But that shit gets old and I really wanted a man. Soon I discovered scriptural literature and it's really helped me in my contentment and peace, those are the two main things you need if you're doing hard time. I also hung around those older sister's, doing life. They kept me motivated to carry on because some were never going to have the chance to see the outside." Teresa stated thoughtfully.

Nancy gave her friend an optimistic gaze and said.

"We're all going to be ok, if we just stop all of this separatism among us… It's hard to get two niggas to go half on 10 piece box of Popeye's chicken. If crackahs stop making drawers today all these niggas will go naked. That business that you want to start I'd like to be down with it, what type of business is it?" Nancy asked.

"While I was in the joint, I learned allot of culinary skills and medical skills. If I can find a little descent building that can hold four tables, I know we'll have a successful restaurant.

I've learn how to make ribs so dope, they'll stop people from buying that shit that they get at those suppose to be rib joints. While I was in school in the Pen, we prepared different dishes for the staff…you know the Warden, a couple of higher ups in corrections and their colleagues who visited the prison. All of the feedback was on my ribs and potato salad. I made a contact with a dorm mate and she informed me of her cousin who could get all of the restaurant equipment I wanted…like fryers, freezers etcetera." Teresa said strongly.

"I'm going to make this shit happen."

"If you want to, you and the kids can move in with me...and we can go half on these bills, at the house...now that it's just me there." Nancy said.

"I spoke with Marcy, and she's going to help me get in at that hospital where she works. I'm a licensed Registered Nurse and I have Surgitech skills. Besides I was missing my children everyday, and really the most valuable thing about being locked up...is that you have time to concentrate on your studies without distractions. I don't think out here, I could have obtained two degrees."

"For real, it's hella distractions out here...I know what you're saying." Nancy commented.

"I'll let Cliff know that I'll be moving in with you, because he's not letting those kids go anywhere. I'll probably have to have visitation with my own children. Aint that's something", as she laughed... "How many women you know that has a brother that loves her kids more than she does?"

"Not many." Nancy answered.

As they were nearing the facility two youths passed them a block away from the NA facility rocking. "WHY'S MY NIGGA ALWAY YELLIN THAT BROKE SHIT, LET'S GET MONEY SON, NOW YOU WANNA SMOKE SHIT...CHILL GOD, YOU KNOW THE SUN DON'T CHILL ALLAH. WHAT'S TODAY'S MATHEMATICS SON, KNOWLEGE GOD". From the 'Only Built for Cubin' LP by Raekwon.

"I think we're here, and I don't want to be late to my livelihood and that's staying clean and sober," Teresa said as she pulled onto the gravel parking lot. The facility was a two story modern styled building that was neatly decorated with plants and 50 cushioned chairs for the attendees, a nice podium for the speaker and huge pictures that lined the walls of directors and people who have ten years or more clean time and are continuing on keeping their lives away from drugs and alcohol.

"This place is huge and it smells so pleasant in here," Teresa stated as they stepped into the facility. There was a beautiful full figured dark skinned lady that stood behind the coffee and snack counter, Nancy and Teresa walked over to the lady to find out if she could locate Ms. Betty Luv for them.

"Ah yes, excuse me Ms., is there a Ms. Betty Luv here?" Nancy asked. Ms. Luv just looked at them both and said.

"Let me check in the back, I'm sure she's around here somewhere. She left for a second and came back and said I'm Ms. Luv may I help the both of you. Nancy laughed and says quickly".
"Hi, How are you, I'm Marcy's friend Nancy, and this here is Teresa."

"How are you ladies doing? Yes, I'm Betty Luv, and this is your home if you have the mindset on success and living free from drugs and alcohol." She continued, "This is a nice place ladies, the coffees free and the snacks are fresh, and we make ready to order sandwiches, whatever you want is back here except chitterlings", she laughed, "Even though I wish we'd serve chitterlings. Anyway there's always someone back here."

Ms. Luv then took them on a tour of the facility.
"Here ladies on the second floor we have a gym and a nursery, for those that are attending the meeting and have children. It's basically community change we're trying to start here. I've always said there is 24 hours in a day and if we can concentrate on addiction as being something that we choose and not something we have to live with, and in addition love and care for each other's needs, then we'll be okay"… she continued. "I've always said that being addicted to crack cocaine is like being in an abusive relationship, you like the good that he or she brings to our lives, but in the end they shoot us with two gun shots to the heart to make sure we're dead. And anybody who's ever smoked Crack knows that's just how it is. "

Teresa was impressed and said nothing, the facility will be ideal for her, since she has two elementary school children, and she's trying not to spend every moment away from them, since she's fresh from being released from prison.

"If you ladies would like to reach me at anytime you can call me at this number or e-mail me, I check them every hour, even if I'm getting my sex on, I'll answer, because that's what we are striving for, supporting each other at all cost." Ms. Luv emphasized strongly.

The ladies stepped down to the first level of the building, and Mr. Norton Kay greeted Ms. Luv with a hug and a kiss.

"Ladies this is Mr. Norton Kay who will be the speaker of this evening's meeting," Ms. Luv stated introducing him. Mr. Kay looks at the ladies and was dressed immaculately in a tailored suit and a pair of eel skinned slippers with ¾ black silk socks on.

"So how are you ladies this fine afternoon?" Norton Kay asked Teresa and Nancy while shaking their hands.

"Very fine sir." Nancy said as Teresa was nodding in agreeance.

"I'm pretty sure that you ladies will be a part of this facility and be a part of our plight for living clean and sober from alcohol and drugs… mainly crack. We're about to get funding from the state, which means jobs, adequately financed employees and job security, which is most important." Norton Kay stated. He continued. "Its past time for us striving for sobriety to support each other, now that we have the means to do so. It's time to make it happen and we're going to make it happen, and this is for all people." Norton Kay optimistically stated.

Ms. Luv smiled as she guided Nancy and Teresa into the room where the meeting would be held. All three of the ladies walked on the beautiful night blue carpet to the front of the hall. Nancy and Teresa took front row seats beside each other as Ms. Luv handed both ladies the syllabus or plans for the up and coming months, then went to her office, at the back of the stage. Norton Kay was in his office adjacent to Ms. Luv's office, preparing his opening presentation for today's meeting.

The members of the home group were flocking in along with 20 or 30 newcomers, they'd needed more seating to accommodate everyone… and they did just that. The message was tolerating the shortcomings we have for ourselves in order to untangle the grip of personal addiction. All were seated and Norton Kay took the stage and Ms. Luv took a front row seat, while Judy and Teresa took their seats towards the middle. There were small microphones on the back of each seat, in case of open discussion.

"How's everyone?" Norton Kay asked rather rambunctiously. The audience smiled and listened attentively on every word that Mr. Kay spoke after that introduction.

"We are here for one reason and that's to get rid of what's been keeping us from having the type of life we need to have." He continued. "Notice that I didn't say the type of life we want to have, but the life each of us need to have. I've been clean from heroin, alcohol, and most recently crack for 15 years now, how did I do it? I did it through prayer and faith. That's it, prayer and faith. I've always believed in God and the scriptures, it's how my Grandmother and mother raised me, so when I became an adult and started to have hard times, addicted to crack, heroin and constantly going to jail. I went back and use my degree in kneeology, and this is the result of getting on your knees and praying even in good times. Look at me, those that know me close, knows that only he, the master, has cleaned me up like this…with a little help from me. Being addicted to crack and heroin is almost like breathing while you're in Satin's pit literally. C'mon now most of ya'll out there know what I'm talking about…Then let me hear ya."

The audience applauded and rose to their feet.

"Are we together on stomping out this madness?"

They responded, yeah!

"Then let's act like it. Everyone that's believes we've all defeated drugs and life threatening addictions give somebody a hug."

Each person hugged the person next to them. The auditorium was packed and there was warmth in the room like a small Pentecostal church on a rainy cold Sunday morning, all was missing was the bent wire hanger, the washboard instrument and the preacher with raspy voice. Mr. Norton Kay continued on.

"Now we're concentrating on meeting everyone's needs here. If you need groceries, childcare, transportation, a job, we'll all come together so that none of us are not lacking in these areas. I want y'all to get numbers and use them. Let's defeat these small things so that we can accomplish bigger things. Dose everyone have a copy of the program and the facilities benefits? Those that don't have a copy raise your hand and one will be given to you right now. Now that we're ready, let's start our open discussion whomever's ready to speak with a concern, standup and address your concern about drug addiction or whatever it is that's complicating you."

Off the Chain was nearly sold out of the product, she had just 3 quarter pieces left and $650.00 cash in her purse, she thought that she would go over to the hotel room to check on Bowler Jack. He was there, lying in the middle of the hotel bed smoking a Newport watching Judge Judy when she opened the door.

Chain closed the door behind her and walked over to the bed and plopped between Jack's legs as if she was a little girl exhausted. Jack pulled her up to him and deeply tasted the inside of her mouth and told her that he missed her and to never stay away from him that long without calling. She smiled and pulled out the wad of cash and plopped it on the bed beside table. Jack's eyes stretched wide and he was speechless on the amount of cash she brought in. Chain layed back on a pillow that rested on the headboard of the bed.

"You see all of that loot there, that's what I'm about, having and not losing a damn thing." Jack looked over at the money, and was thanking God that he met her.

"Damn baby, you handle your business, you did what you said you were going to do." Jack said admiringly.

"That's what it's all about isn't it, doing it and not talking it. I'm a big girl so I do big girl things…and you're taking your ass to work tomorrow, Right?"

"Yes… and I really want you to move in with me and my roommate. We share a nice 2,400 sq. ft. place with a deck on the back. Besides, we've been really talking about getting a feminine aura around the place, and that's going to be you baby. I really feel that you are for my benefit. As far as my roomy goes, he's cool, he's a welder and makes about 50k a year, and doesn't have any biological kids. His only downfall is that he's in love with this chick that has three kids, and he stays smoking pounds of weed, talking shit about her fucking around on him. I hope you can talk some sense in his head. It's pathetic he's taking care of her and her kids and all of the single women are out here with jobs and no kids, that will make him a good partner."

Chain just sat there listening.

"I would tell him all of time, man you don't have to sit crying over this woman, even though she's attractive as hell, I'm not going to lie, but it's not worth what he's putting up with. She got him whipped." Jack said.

"Yeah, it sounds like he's a good dude that needs to hang out with us. We need to take him to the club over on the Avenue; there are nothing but women with careers and homes up in there. They are looking for a descent man to spend time with." Chain stated.

"Sounds to me like that's the perfect spot for my partner." Jack said.
"Yeah, man let me get in that shower so we can break out of here." Chain quipped.
As Jack smacked her on her naked ass and lit a Newport cigarette, he layed back on the bed with his legs crossed and the two pillows fluffed between his head and the head board, and started having thoughts of Love. He decided right then and there that he would never pick up another crack rock and smoke it. His new goal would be that he'll constantly be about the solution not about the problem.

Chain stepped out of the shower and Jack greeted her with a kiss.

"Baby, I picked up everything, so all we have to do is walk out the door." Jack said.

"Yeah, I'm just going to slip on these jeans, because I need to get some clean underwear, and I'm hungry I need a slice of pizza from that little place in the mall that has the best tasting pizza."

"Yeah… I know where you are talking about." Jack stated.

They both stepped out of the hotel room and got into Jack's truck, and headed for the mall as he inserted the 'Jewels' CD by OC, "HE LIVED THE LIFE OF A HUSTLER, NOT SYMPATHETIC TO A USER." The track was Hypocrite.

"Turn that down a little." Chain offered.

All the while, Trevor Karp was in his cell talking with his cellmate.

"Man, it really makes me feel good that you are being released… my old ass will be stuck up in here for a while." Macklin said with a tone of sad admiration in his voice.

"Man, don't you even sweat that, it's we're being released because if it wasn't for you none of this would be possible. I'm going to write you all the time and I know this thick fine female I'm going to hook you up with, and she'll visit you and write you also, so that you can do this time easy, because without you man, none of this would be possible." Trevor stated.

"Yeah, that sounds nice," Macklin added.

The prison board had sent all of Trevor's information back to the local authorities stating of his being released. Skip's file ended up on the top judge's desk. The judge read the file and realized that the prison authorities had made a mistake. The main file of Attempted Murder against Ms. Nancy Taylor was never sent to the prison. The local Judge immediately got on the phone, and called the prison authorities.

"Hello, Florida State prison system, this is Mike Cobb director of the prison… how my I help you?"

"Yes Mr. Cobb, this is Judge Louise Drayton, how are you today?"

"I'm fine judge, how may I may I help you?"

"There is a mistake that was made on Trevor Karp to be released, he is not to be released as I'm speaking to you, because he doesn't qualify." She continued. He has a violent charge of attempted murder in his jacket; the file didn't make it to your prison. I'm faxing it ASAP, so you can have a look at it." The judge stated.

"Great judge I'll be expecting it, and will act on this promptly, because Mr. Trevor Karp was one of the ones that we were going to release first. The file we received was the drug conviction, but I really appreciate this judge. We will get on this pronto and we'll double check all of the files that come to my office…thank you."

"No problem and if you have any questions about any of those that are going to be released look at the total jacket in detail, they have to look over each file in detail… that's what we pay them for." said the Judge, then she hung up the phone.

veryone was participating in this NA meeting. Sharing their thoughts and how they felt about drug abuse and addiction. One Mexican female express her plight so sublime that the entire room stood and gave her a standing ovation. Her name is Makita and she shared that she sold everything out of her house even her children's baby bottles to get another hit. Eventually she had lost everything, and was presently at the homeless shelter and was looking for a place to live. Mr. Norton Kay ordered one of the ushers to pull her out of crowd and set her up for housing. As he closed the meeting, he said.

"Now sister Makita is not the only one in this shape from smoking crack. It doesn't make a difference people; we just have to leave the total activity of drug usage alone, stop it, leave it, and run from crack as if you're running for your life. Right Now, let's keep it tight and together. We can do that with each others' help, y'all take care." There were applause.

The meeting ended and everyone hugged and exchange numbers. Teresa and Nancy met with Ms. Luv and Mr. Norton Kay; they discuss the two young ladies getting involved in the program and becoming leaders on the plight of staying clean and developing a better community.

Tonya was back in Atlanta living her life with her two kids, who are now 12 and 15. The young man, Mack is 12 and the young lady Tracy is 15. Tracy has been acting out, bringing home bad grades, and the rumor is out that she is sexually active and recently she was temporarily suspended from school for fighting. Tonya had been talking with her to give her the benefit of the doubt; because she has been a mother of old school values (Beat and punish first, then talk it out later). This particular morning she went to work, her son Mack had went to school and Tracy was home on suspension.

Tonya, she serves as vice principal at one of the top high schools in the Atlanta area academically and athletically it's the Duke University of high schools, 99.2% graduation rate. Three years in a row state champs in basketball and football. She is highly admired by students and staff alike.

It was about 10am or so Tracy had invited a 19 year old high school drop out over to the house and they were in Tracy's room having sex. Tonya had forgot a very important disc and needed to double back to the house. She turned the key and stepped into the house. There was laughter and moaning sounds coming from Tracy's upstairs bedroom. Tonya quietly and calmly walked up to her daughter's room and opened the door. The young man's head was buried between Tracy's legs.

Tracey was shocked and terrified, mainly because of her mother's reaction. Tonya closed the door and picked up the disc and headed back to work. She didn't react hysterically or anything, was sort of musing to herself on her way back to work.

"I can't believe this lil bitch." Tonya mused to herself as she pulled into the school's parking lot.

Tracy knew she was in trouble, and told the young man to put on his clothes and leave. Tracy led the guy downstairs and out of the door. She locked the door, went back upstairs, through on her satin robe with a thong underneath and just layed in her bed thinking of the what her mother's actions were going to be towards her.

All the while Tonya was thinking of the punishment she was going to inflict upon Tracy. Tonya weighed the options, and decided to call her attorney boyfriend Pete about the situation.

"Well baby you have to look at this for what it really is, always look at situations with you benefiting from it, she's 15, and she'll make many mistakes in her life. You have to handle this to where you want get yourself into any trouble. Eventually she'll change for the better. She knows that you'll bust her ass open for whatever, she knows you don't play." Tonya just listened to Pete as he spoke plainly, as he continued.

"Baby she's not a little girl anymore, handle it with that perspective. Set her up with counseling and monitored punishment, but keep her as your daughter and friend, that will work and you'll keep your daughter and your freedom. You know I need you out here for my doses of intimacy." Pete said.

Tonya thought deep and smiled saying, "Alright, when will I see you?"

"Baby I want to see you soon, I'm coming to pick you up for lunch, say about twelve." Pete stated.

"Yeah twelve will be fine. I'm really in the mood for some fresh oysters." She stated.

"I'll pick you up at twelve and we can go to that 'Oyster Bistro'." Pete told her as he hung up the phone.

Tracy on the other hand was worried to death about what her mother was going to do to her. She walked around the house, prayed, watched TV, cleaned and swept the house about 10 times, hoping that her mother wouldn't kill her when she comes home from work.

All the while Trevor Karp was in the cell with Macklin just talking about life on the outside and eating good food and being free.

"Open up cell 42," the officer stated. He continued. "Trevor Karp get squared away, you're going to see the Warden."

Karp tucked his prison issued shirt inside of his pants and walked out of the cell. With an officer escorting him, he was full of optimism, knowing that he was going to be a free man soon. He walked with his chest out as he passed the cells, down a narrow corridor which led to the Wardens office. The officer opened the door, he let Karp in first then he entered with his hand on his revolver. The Warden then spends around in the leather 'Ox Blood' red office recliner.

"Mr. Karp, have a seat."
Karp sat down.

"Do you remember a woman by the name of Nancy Taylor?" The Warden asked.

"No, I don't know her, sir." Karp said sharply.

"Well, I really apologize for this, but the Judge in your home town that's handling your case for being released said that you nearly murdered a Nancy Taylor, do you remember that?"

"No. I qualify for being released right?" Karp asked nervously

The Warden paused and looked Karp squarely in the eye, and said no. Karp erupted, shoving all of the Warden's paper work and desk ornaments to the floor. The officer, who was in pretty good shape, slammed Karp to the floor and cuffed him. Trevor Karp was shuffled and secured in a padded cell, stripped naked until he could conform. He was in that padded cell for three days, and then moved to a maximum secured cell block, where there was one prisoner to a cell.

"All ya'll are bitches, trying to play me for a joke."He constantly lamented through the hand sized opening in the steel cell door.

Karp gnashed his teeth and banged his head against the steel door until he bled. One officer heard and saw him do this and said to another officer.
"Look at that suicidal motherfucker, he's going to crack his head opened because they want let him out to play." The officer stated.

Then one of the officers who felt a little sympathy towards Karp, walked up to the cell and told one of the guards to open up the cell, as he went in. He embraced Karp and said…

"Man, I know how you feel, they are going to try to get that mid-evil torture chair for you to sit in if you don't conform and I know you don't want that, you don't have to do yourself like this my brother.

Regardless if you maim yourself or hang yourself, you're going to do the time. I've been through the same, use to be on the daily, losing jobs, arguments and fights with the wife when I come home, but I reacted positively through all of it. I maintained self. I believed in me, therefore all of the obstacles I'm faced with, I can handle them, because I know who I am and where I've got to go." The officer said.

Karp had calmed down, and relaxed. The officer stood at the entrance of the cell door and said,

"Karp man, it's not what you get out of life, but what you put into it".

The officer then ordered the guard in the control booth to lock the cell. Trevor sat there, confused and bewildered, then he thought that he'd have to make the most out being incarcerated for nearly the rest of his life. He looked to his right and there was a book lying on the side of his bunk that the correctional officer had left, it was entitled the 'Black Holocaust'. He picked it up and started reading it. The introduction of the book was interesting, it read.

'Of all the rhetoric that is given to the burning of the Jews by the Germans and other treatment of man's inhumanity towards his fellow man, there is nothing that can hold a light to the slavery of African people for 400 years in the United States of America.'

Trevor started reading the book, and as he turned each page he started getting knowledge of self, which was totally stripped from the African when they were brought to the western hemisphere in the late 1600's. Not knowing who you are and what is your purpose for living or being, and made and trained to depend on the plantation owners and other whites. Chained and restricted to only the lowest of life's essentials to exist on, daily and nightly. The process damaged the African so much till it directly affected his and her seeds when they were born. The seed would naturally think that servitude and being dependent of another was his or her birthright, to live a life of servitude; slavery.

A meal was brought for him to eat, and that book stayed in his face. It let him know that if blacks could survive slavery in America for 400 plus years, he could do his part by at least living. Karp started thinking deep on why he chose to sell drugs in the first place. All of the good opportunities that we have today and we're not taking advantage of them. A black can go to any hotel and have a stay, go to any restaurant and have a meal without being seated to the back of a restaurant. They can shop freely, unlike his great grandparents in the 30's and 40's. He remembered what his grandfather told him before he died. His grandfather told him—"Son your decisions and choices you make as a man, effects every part of your being. You can't serve two masters either you hate one and love the other." He suddenly came to the realization that he played his ownself.

Karin Sa'llah, aka Off the Chain, was raised in a Nation of Islam household. Her mother and dad were benevolent friends of the Minister Malcolm X. In the eighteen years growing up in the household, she particularly remembers her dad stressing to her that in order to survive at any time: One must have knowledge of self, and everything else exists around that.

She and Bowler Jack had just gotten in late, Jack's roommate and friend Adam Kessler was over to his lady friend Brenda's house. Adam had just spent $250 at Wal-Mart for groceries and $150 dollars in the mall for Brenda and her four children, none which are his, Adam has no kids. He leaves Jack a message on their answering machine.

'YO MAN, THIS ME. I'M OVER AT BRENDA'S, I WON'T BE IN TONIGHT, AND LOOK ON TOP OF THE REFRIGERATOR, THAT LIGHT BILL IS DUE. I'LL TAKE THEM HALF DOWN THERE TO KEEP THE SERVICE ON... LATER'.

Off the Chain was totally taken by the house and how clean it was, and the grade of expensive furniture that was in the house which mainly belong to Adam when he use to travel overseas to do under water welding for the United States Government.

"Baby I'll make you lunch for tomorrow morning and sit it on the counter. Go and hit that shower and bed, so you can get some shut eye."

Jack went to the linen closet and didn't say a word just got a shower and got in the bed. Chain made his lunch, looked all through the house, took her shower and smoked a cigarette on the back deck, by the time she made it to the bed Jack was knocked out. Sleeping lovely. Soon she followed suit.

All the while Adam was sleep in Brenda's bed, it was about 2 am and Adam was dead sleep. Brenda quietly got out the bed without awaking Adam, and went to the kitchen and got her cell phone out of the cabinet, then proceeded to call this guy Greg, who she is cheating on Adam with.

"Hello."

"What you doing?" Brenda asked.

"Nothing", Greg responded.

"What's up with you?"

"I'm waiting for you to come in the morning and eat this."

"Yo…where that nigga at?"

"Oh, he's knocked out, I bought you some groceries with his money, and I got the crawfish you like also."

"Oh yeah, thank you baby, I appreciate it, I was in the bed getting rest for our little venture tomorrow morning when that nigga leave the house." Greg said.

"OK, baby get some sleep."

"Alright bye." The guy said, then hung up.

Brenda went back to bed.

It was soon morning a Bowler Jack had gotten dressed and walked through the kitchen on his way out of the house to grab the bagged lunch that Chain had made for him and was headed out, but before he left he went back to the bedroom and watched her as she slepted. He then knew that he was in love with her. He leaned over and gave her a kiss on her forehead then, left out of the house and went to work.

Adam went to work as well. The shut down he was working on was at the St. Mane Power Park. Adam was one of the head welders and ran a crew of ten. His partner Will was an experienced welder as well, but wasn't quite the welder Adam was. Will was a little older than Adam and always kidded him about taking care of Brenda's kids that weren't his.

"Boy what's happening with that girl and all those kids she's got?"
Adam looked at Will, and laughed.
"She's alright, old man."
"Hey Adam, I don't want to get all into your business and shit like that, but what's the deal with the children's daddies."
"She don't know and can't find any of them, I take care of them man because I love her."

"Boy, you gonna get enough of that I love you shit, and being hypnotized by ass and titties. Young blood, I remember when I was in my twenties I had a bitch that was fine as hell troop, she had five kids from three different daddies. Man I'll be at her house in the evening eating dinner and niggas would knock on the door asking where their kid is and shit, man I got tired of that shit and left that night. She tried that calling me, and I told her the only way I fuck wit a bitch that has kids, the nigga got to be either dead or doing prison time for about sixty years."

"God damn, boy you crazy than a motherfuckah." Adam said as he kept laughing.

"Nah man, that's real shit, it hurt a little bit, to let her go, but two weeks had passed and I got my check and bust it and had an ass pocket full of money. The teller counted out to me so much money till her wrist started hurting; she had to get a wrist brace. She was fine as hell too Jack, so I asked her out, and guess what she said?"

"What?"

"She said yeah nigga, that's my wife to this day, she didn't have any kids, smart as fuck and she can cook, love to cook and clean my nigga." Will stated.

"Damn that's cool, I'm happy for you nigga, now let's get some of this shit welded around here." Adam stated since he was the supervisor.

Brenda's house was clear. The kids were off to school and she put on some tight white silk panties and a bra to hold her nearly perfect breast in. Her cell phone ranged.

"Hello."
"Ya house clear?" Greg asked.
"Yeah, said Brenda just c'mon on in, the door will be unlocked."
"Cool," said Greg as he closed his cell phone.
Brenda was in her bedroom; she lit a couple of incense, then spread out on her mattress and was watching one of the court shows. Greg parked on the street in front of the house. He walks up to the door and let himself in. Greg locked the door behind him and walked to Brenda's room. She was lying across her bed on her stomach. Her ass was heavily accentuating through the white translucent panties she wore. Greg approached the bed and they went at it.

All the while Adam was about to call for lunch, he was quite hungry and thought since he'd bought Brenda's groceries last night he could get a bite there, plus he was feeling the urge to see her. Adam's partner and co-worker Will said.

"Yo Adam, we're going down there to that Bar- be- que joint down the street to get a bite... yo man, you coming?"

"Nah man, I got some food, y'all go on ahead, and I'll see y'all in an hour."

Adam was in love with Brenda and he started having this bad feeling in his stomach. A sort of sickly feeling. He got into his truck and headed over to her house. He pulled into the driveway and saw a strange car parked on the road in front of her house. He had a key so he let himself in. There was music playing as he walked down the hall to her room. He opened the door and Brenda's legs were in the air, her ass cheeks were lifted off of the mattress and Greg was pounding inside of her, as she expressed.

"Oh shit, ahh baby...just like that...damn."

Adam's heart fell to the floor as he immediately closed the door. Adam quickly walked back to the kitchen all that was racing in his mind was to murder both of them, but then he'd have to do time. Then he thought 'Crime of Passion,' but he wasn't married to her. Brenda heard the slam of the door and pushed Greg off of her, grabbed her robe that was lying in the bedside chair and walked out into the hall, she saw that it was Adam and walked slowly towards him, the guy stayed in the room, trying to put his clothing on as quickly as possible. Adam grabbed the bread and lunch meat, along with the gigantic bag of crawfish and all of the snack juices for her kids out of the refrigerator, then headed for the door. Brenda tried to explain saying.

"Baby, it's not what you think!"

Adam made it out of the house without saying a word to Brenda, cranked his truck up and headed back to the job. All he could think about passing the cars on his way back to the job was that another man was sexing the woman he loved. Brenda went back into the bedroom and sat on the edge of the bed, thinking of what just occurred. Greg has no job and no money in the bank, he lives with his uncle, and he really doesn't have anything. The two men are totally opposite, one has and the other doesn't have a damn thing. All of this raced in Brenda's mind as Greg tried to grab the back of her shoulders as if to comfort her, she pushed him away. Brenda looked at him with so much annoyance you could have cut her anger and disappointment from her skin with a knife. She held her face in her hands and told him.

"Please get out my face and my house… Now!"

Adam got back to work and put on his welding equipment, and tried to weld. He couldn't. Will, could see that something very bad was bothering Adam, he looked as if he had seen the worst nightmare manifested in real life. Will decided not to say anything, and then Adam's cell phone ranged.

'ADAM BABY, I REALLY DIDN'T MEAN', Then there was sudden click on Brenda's phone line, Adam had hung the phone up on her. Brenda flung the cell phone to the bed and thought of what she'd lost. She thought of her kids' medical care. When one of her kids had gotten sick, she would call Adam, and he'd bring her his medical insurance card, Adam had them on his plan. Whenever she needed groceries, light bill paid, rent, he would be there for her, now all of that had ended.

Adam's 2'oclock break had come. He wasn't feeling that good so he told the fellows that Will would be in charge; Adam needed to take a break. It was as if his world had caved in, catching another man sexing the woman he deeply cared for. He caught the elevator down to ground level and went into the break trailer, poured a cup of coffee and called the house hoping that someone would answer. Jack was there. He'd gotten off work early so that he and Chain could take the day shopping and look for an NA meeting near them. The phone ranged.

"Hello." Chain greeted.
"Hello how are you ma'am, is Jack there?"
"Hold on", Chain said as she handed Jack the phone.
"What's happening man, this me, Adam."
"Yeah, what's happening, Cool?" Jack addressed.
"Man, I don't know what to do; I caught her in the bed today with some dude." Adam stated.
"Oh shit, are you alright, man?"
"After all I did for that bitch and her kids and she does this shit to me, man, I can't even stand up, let alone work."

Bowler Jack paused in sympathy for his friend and roommate then spoke.
"Adam get off work and come to the house man, I've got something for you."
"What?"

"I'm taking you out for an oyster and lobster dinner then afterwards we're going to a club. Ka'rin who's staying with us now told me about this club near the Bluff, she says that allot of single career women cool out there; we need to dot up in there and have a drink…you know man something to get your mind off of that bullshit. You can get loose and check it out. They are your caliber of ladies anyway. I never could figure out what you were doing with that foot dragger in the first place. But for real…now is the time to be around some people that love and care for you man." Jack explained.

"Man I appreciate that."

"Adam man you know that aint know thang, because I know you'll do the same for me. Hey Adam whatever you do man, don't go around there, that's real shit man. Going back around her is only going to make that shit worse…c'mon to the house."

"Alright man let me go and tell the guys what I want done, and I'll be there shortly."

"Alright later." Jack said as he hung up the phone.
Jack walked out on the back balcony and lit a Newport, Chain followed him. He sat down and took a long drag, paused for a sec, and said.

"I told you that bitch wasn't shit. He caught her in bed with another dude today. We're taking him to that Club you told me about."

"Is he alright?" she asked.
"Yeah, he'll be alright, I told him to come straight to the house. Let me get in this shower."
"Alright." Chain offered.
"We can stop by the mall and pick out a nice dress and heels for you to where on our way out tonight.
"I'll do you one better. I've already got a nice dress and nylons with the seams the hold nine."
"Damn when'd you do that?"
"About a couple of hours after you left this morning. I cleaned the house, washed up and called a cab so I could do some shopping…I got you something too."
"Oh yeah."

They both left the deck, they took a shower together, then Jack went to the closet pulled out nice pair of dress slacks a silk shirt and a pair of black Stacy Adams. He flung the clothing in a chair in the bedroom and Chain came behind him and handed a bottle of Karl Lagerfeld cologne the original fragrance.

"Hey, baby, I've been looking all over for a bottle of this." Jack said of the cologne, as Chain grabbed the nylons and garter belt out of the dresser drawer. She sat on the edge of the bed and started putting them on, along with some tight fitting panties that accentuated every crevice of her vagina mound. Jack was mesmerized; he had never watched a woman get dressed before he started getting an erection just watching Karin aka Off the Chain getting dressed. Ten minutes had passed and they were fully dress, and sipping Hennessey on the back deck.

Adam pulled into the driveway, and let himself in the house. He didn't see anyone in any part of the house as he went through a couple of rooms. He walked toward the deck, opened the sliding glass doors and stepped out onto the deck. Jack got up from his seat and gave his partner a hug, while Chain stayed seated.

"Yo Adam you alright, you look good though." Jack stated embracing his friend.
Adam looked like he had been in a war.
"Yeah, I'll be alright."
"Oh man I apologize bra, this is my girl, Karin and Karin this is Adam." Jack pronounced, while Adam and Chain extended a hand toward each other for a handshake.
"Oh, and she's going to be living with us."
"Ok", Adam calmly said.
"Hey man, go on and get ready, we're leaving in a half an hour." Jack expressed.

Adam went back into the house, went to his room, took off his work clothes and grabbed a robe. He sat on the edge of the bed, looked into his mirror, which hung the wall length of the bed. He wondered how he was such a fool and then realized what his mother had told him when he was about 19. She said, 'Baby don't ever give your strength to a woman. And if one hurt you get up and go find another one.'

That direct thought lingered in his head as he got up walked to the shower that was connected to his room. He unrobed, got in the shower and prayed while the water beat on his back. He got out the shower, dried off, got dressed and went into the livingroom where Jack and Chain sat on the sofa, watching the nightly news.

"Boy you ready?"

"Yeah"

He sat down, looked at Chain and asked.

"How are you ma'am?"

"I'm fine Adam." Chain answered respectfully.

"I was just telling Jacquel the other night, that we needed a female around here, and I'm not saying that to be chauvinistic."Adam stated in a cool tone.

Chained just looked and smiled, she knew that prayer and faith would get you whatever you wanted, but she never knew that God could work that fast on her behalf, just a couple of days ago, she was a strung-out, a struggling addict, living on the street. . Now she felt that her life had meaning. She met a good guy with a nice home and seems to be real cool.

The three of them got up and headed outside to Jack's SUV.

The mood was quiet on their way to the restaurant. They were seated at a booth.

"Welcome to Light House Bay, and what will you guys have to drink tonight?" The waitress asked.

Adam and Jack waited for Chain to order first.

"I'll have Pepsi with light ice." Chain stated to the waitress.

"I think I'll go with the Bloody Mary heavy on the Ciroc and Tabasco". Jack said.

"I'll have a Pepsi light ice." Adam ordered.

The waitress went to get the drinks, then returned shortly afterwards. Are you all ready to order?" They looked around at each other and Chain said.

"I'll have the Walnut salad and fried grouper along with dozen oysters and gator tail for an appetizer."

"I'll have the Main lobster a dozen of fresh ice-cold clams." Jack stated.

Adam looked over the menu and looked at Jack.

"Cuz, get whatever you want man, when I said I was taking you out, I meant just that… it's all about you tonight brother, just remember that." Jack forcefully explained.

"Cool. I'll have two dozen of the select oysters on the half shell ice-cold, two Main Lobsters and a bowl of oyster gumbo." Adam said looking up at the attractive young waitress.

The waitress jotted the orders down and thanked them for visiting the restaurant. "Is there anything else yu'all would like?"

"Nah, I'm good." Jack stated.

"I fine, thank you."

"So am I", Adam followed.

The waitress told them to enjoy. They were taking in the ambiance of the restaurant; Adam was gazing at the fish in the aquarium when the silence broke.

"Jack, you believe that?… I mean all I wanted for her was to be comfortable, along with her kids".

"Adam that shit aint nothing but a blessing, you aint no scrub or chump… you know you don't need a foot dragger, you need someone that's going to compliment you, man." Jack said.

They sat around the booth just admiring the decor, until Adam asked the question.

"So how'd ya'll meet?"

Jack didn't want to reveal exactly how he and Chain had met, so he said…

"Man we met at a convenience store, she was getting her lottery ticket and I was trying to explain to the man behind the register to stop trying to shit people out of their money. He must've been doing that shit for quite awhile, but I know the nigga shorted me on my money, plenty of times. That Arab store a block away from that fish market, those some motherfuckahs in there boy…everything in that store is a dollar more than the other stores…I try not to go in that bitch for nothing, then I saw her and the rest is history…you see how she looks, it aint hard to tell, Huh man?" Jack heavily admitted with a smile, while putting an arm around Ka'rin.

Adam laughed as he was looking at Chain…admiring her natural womanly beauty. Chain just sat next to Jack enjoying the fried gator tail.

"Man, that's all right." Adam complimented.

"Yo, we're taking you to that split level club Karin was telling me about with all those eligible women. Boy I haven't been clubbing in a while, for sure I can't wait to get there and I know you can't either. Single ladies with careers and jobs…get into a different environment man, instead of staying stagnant and feeling that that's all you deserve. Adam this is a big world that God made for man and woman to enjoy… venture out and live man! Be flexible Adam, and get out of that habit of immobilization!" Jack heavily expressed.

"Yeah, but Jack I'm proud of you man. You know when we get up in the age we're in. We need a female at our side at all times." Adam acknowledged.

"But it's got to be a good one my brother." Jack retorted, as the waitress was placing the plates and platters on the table.

"Will there be anything else?" The waitress asked.

"Nah, I'm alright. Oh could you bring me water with ice and a couple slices of fresh lemon?" Jack asked.

"Another Pepsi for me," Chain offered.

"A sweet tea for me." Adam added.

"Alright", the waitress said as she walked off.

Jack had already bust open a Lobster claw, and had to use a napkin quick, because of the juices that was flowing from it. Adam had devoured nearly a dozen of the oysters on the half-shell, as Chain was cutting into her giant mushrooms stuffed with rib-eye and melted provolone cheese.

They finished their dinners, sat back and engaged in light conversation about how the food was, then Jack and Adam laid five dollars a piece on the table for the waitress.

"Got damn, that food was the best I've ever eaten at a restaurant. The food was so good I almost climaxed," Chain whispered in Jack's ear.

"Alright now." Jack added.

They walked out the restaurant sat on the benches outside of the establishment. Each fired up a cigarette. The lights from other establishments and the cars passing on the highway were accentuating the night sky.

"Yo, that club is red hot!" Chain exclaimed as she continued. "I haven't been there in a while, but my girl Glow runs it, and if it's anything like the last time I was there, man that's the place to be. Now that the economy is back in order...we've got a brother who's the most powerful man in the world as far as society's standards are concerned and women just feel good at this time." Chain expressed.

"Well let's go, I need to see this piece of heaven that you're talking about." Jack said as they got into the SUV.

Jack switched on the ignition. 'HEY YO SLASH YOUR POSITION, VERBAL MIC PHYSICIAN, BLOW LINES LIKE CHIMES IN A KITCHEN. GOD SHA VEGAS, YOU WANNA STOMP THAT FAKE OUT WHAT, HE BITE EVERYTHING, BITE THESE NUTS.'

"Yo man, that's my 'Immobarlarity' I've been looking for it." Adam said, as Jack looked at him through the rear view mirror with smile on his face.

"Yo, turn that down a little baby, so I can tell you how to get there." Chain stated. She continued. "Make a right at this light, and when you get to the third light that's Argyle make a left there. You'll see the lights and parked cars in parking lot." As they made the left at the street that the club was on, Adam phone rings. Chain and Jack heard it, as Jack turned the volume down.

"Hello."

"Hey baby." It was Brenda, Adam still loved her. She was hurting, knowing that Adam was out of her life. She felt as if her left arm had been cut off. She realized that the little fling she had didn't benefit her in no way. Greg didn't have anything to offer her and she knew it, but Adam did and it was too late.

"Yeah what's up?" Adam asked, instead of hanging up.

"Aint nothing, baby I missed you." Brenda retorted, as Adam switched it to speaker phone so that Jack and Chain could hear her. Jack was a block from the Club and pulled on the side of the road and cut the truck off. Jack looked at Adam seriously through the rear view mirror. Adam sensed that he needed to hang up the phone. He did. Then Jack fired up the ignition and proceeded to head to the packed parking lot of the club.

They pulled into the lot and parked, got out of the truck and entered the club. There was a mix of club music and hardcore 'digging in the crates' style of hip hop. 'I WANT YOUR LOVE' by Chic vibrating the club's wall's. The lighting of the club was first class. The blues, reds, purples, oranges and yellows was scintillating to the eyes and spirit. They made their way to the bar. Chain and Jack sat next to each other and there was a lady by the name of Samantha that was at the bar sipping on sprite and Grenadine, Adam took his seat next to her. The bartender placed himself in front of Adam and he ordered looking at Samantha rather lasciviously.

"Ahh yeah, I'll have what she's drinking,"

Samantha has an alluring beauty; her body is thickly well proportioned. She glanced at Adam from the corner of her eye with a slight smile on her face. The Bartender brought Adam his drink and took the fifty dollar bill that Adam had placed on the counter.

"Oh, I'm Adam; it's nice to meet you." He stated as he took a large gulp of the cold mixed drink.

"Nice to meet you Adam," Samantha said as she gave him a very perceptive look. "Oh, they call me Sammi."

"So, how are you?"

Samantha looked at him with a glare of autonomy, she paused and stated.

"I'm fine.

"So how's this place?" Adam asked.

"Look around you, every woman in here is beautiful and this is my hang out…this is where I come to unwind, so what do you do for a living?" Sammi asked.

"I'm a head welder at that power plant off of New Berlin… and what do you do?"

"I'm a Judge." Sammi said taking a sophisticated sip from her glass.

Adam nearly choked on his on his drink as he signaled to the bartender to bring him another drink, but make it a triple shot of that Finland Ice mountain Vodka…bet?" Adam stated to the bartender.

"So are you married?" He asked.

"No, I'm quite single, no kids… my profession is my family for now. What about you?"

"Same… my job is mines."

They both looked at each other and the DJ put the needle on 'Sweet Thing' by Chaka Kahn.

"Would you like to dance?"

"Well yes". Sammi answered.

They hit the lighted dance floor and embraced. They looked at each in the face then slow danced through the entire song without a word.

Jack and Chain watched from the bar.

"You're right about this place; it's everything you said it was about". Jack said to Chain as Adam and Sammi made their way back to the bar.

"Bartender let me get triple Hennessy straight lots of ice, and the lady would have… what are you having baby?" Adam asked.

"I'll have a double Ciroc with lime and light on the ice." Sammi stated.

As the bartender placed their drinks in front of them, Jack asked.

"Can I call you?... I would like to take you to dinner this week?"

Samantha gave him a card that read SUPERIOR COURT JUDGE-SAMANTHA JENKINS, with her business and cell number in the bottom right corner.

Adam took the card in put into his shirt pocket.

"Samantha I'm glad I met you, you have really made this man have hope, and Ms. Jenkins I'm going to do everything in my power to make you my lady. Who would've thought that I'll have a chance at a judge?"

"You see Adam it's not about titles with most sisters, they just want a man that's going to be responsible and loving...well at least I do. You seem like a good catch and I'm looking forward to your call later in the week."

Jack and Chain were admiring Adam's swagger and was well pleased that he had met someone. They knew that Adam had made a connection, because he stayed around Samantha all night and didn't leave her side. As the club was closing he walked Samantha to her Benz and gave her a long hug and an open mouth kiss, which she did not reject. As she got into her car, Adam leaned inside of her window, she had the S.O.S. Band's 'Do you still want to' on low volume.

"Call me tonight if you're up, OK." Samantha said.

"Alright Ms. Jenkins, see ya." Adam stated as she sped off.

Teresa had landed the job at the second biggest hospital in the Region where her good friend Marcy is employed and Marcy was the main reason Teresa was hired. A month had past and Teresa's promptness and job performance was instrumental in Marcy receiving a raise from 40 thousand a year to 50 thousand. Teresa who did it all from Respiratory therapy to assisting the Nurses in the Nursing department, made overtime weekly and her money was really stacking up. She and Nancy were housemates and they were making it to meetings on the regular. Nancy was working part time at the juvenile facility and supervising at the distribution center for a major chain, where Teresa was supposed to have applied at first, Teresa figured that the comfortable hospital setting would be more to her liking than working in a hot warehouse packing orders.

Marcy and Teresa had just gotten off work and were pulling up in Nancy's drive-way, Teresa's kids were at her brother's house, and the kids were being watched by her brother's girlfriend. Marcy pulled into the driveway. She and Teresa got out of the car and walked up the three small steps, that was surrounded by a beautifully kept yard. Teresa put her key in the door, then her and Marcy entered.

"Nan, where are you!?" Teresa shouted through the house while looking for her in each room, Marcy took a seat on the living room couch and switched on the news. Teresa walked back to the front of the house.

"She's nowhere in the house, I've looked all over, I hope she's not back out there, she was off work 2 hours ago."

Nancy had caught the Greyhound out of town to her parent's house to get her College diploma from Dartmouth College an Ivy League school where she received a degree in business. She also wanted to pick up her credits for an associate degree she earned for teaching. Nancy had gotten tired of looking at herself as low, when she came to the realization that she had more education and certification than the people who were signing her checks.

She had left work early that day, caught the city bus to the Greyhound station and headed for the nearby town where she grew up. Her plan was to stop slaving in the hot warehouse and get into what she went to school for. She had already submitted a resume to one of the local high schools. One of the principal's secretaries of that school left a message on Nancy's answering service, telling her to come in for an interview with the principal.

Her and her Mom are the best of friends. Nancy stayed out of contact with them because she was heavily into smoking crack and she didn't want her parents to know anything about her usage, they knew her like they knew themselves, she is their daughter. So she had no contact until she had gotten clean. Nancy and her mother were watching the 'News hour with Jim Lehrer', when her Father walked in the screened door.

"Who is this, is that my baby?" Nancy's father asked, whom she hadn't seen in years. Nancy sprung up from the couch from where she sat, and bounced into her Dad's arms.

"Girl where you been? Me and your momma been worried to death over you, you look good… stand back let daddy look at you."

Mr. Taylor had just come in from playing golf. He and his lovely wife of 40 years are retired educators. Nancy stood back and let her dad look at her, then she embraced him again as they both went to sit back down on the couch.

"So baby girl, what flew you in?"

"Nothing daddy, I came to get all of my transcripts from college and my diploma, I'm tired of working hard in that warehouse for little or no money. I'm wasting my time and life there", she continued. "One of the local high schools would like for me to come in for an interview. I just want something more satisfying for myself right now."

Her mother prepared the dinner, baked chicken, macaroni and cheese and collards.

"That was a fantastic dinner momma; I'm going to start visiting more often, how's my little sister?"

The mood had suddenly gotten quiet. Nancy's younger sister had nearly terrorized her parents with her Methamphetamine and Ecstasy addiction. Nancy's Father has twice had to fire off his rifle at her friends who were attempting to rob Mr. Taylor and his wife at late hours in the night. Daphne Taylor is Nancy's only sibling and is 15 years younger than Nancy. Daphne is 25 now. She was kicked out the Navy boot camp and never completed her college education, a smart young woman but she never garnered the strength to continue on. There was something about Daphne that's related to nearly everyone who fall victim to substance abuse, they seem to lack inner strength, they're usually the type of people that give up easily when there is a bump in the road, they seem to fall victim to that first bump and give up on life.

"That girl, we don't want anything to do with her. She's not even welcomed here No more." Mr. Taylor said, with a look of seriousness and sadness in his eyes.

"We raised her right, gave her everything she wanted and needed and she turns out like this."

There was a sudden knock on the door, almost a desperate bamming knock as if someone was desperately trying knock down the door.

B-doom, B-doom, was the sound of the assault rifle.

They all raced to the door, Mr. Taylor opened it and there it was, his youngest daughter sprawled out on his front porch, with a hole in her back so big that it nearly decapitated her head from the rest of her body. Daphne Taylor was shot trying to rob a Meth lab, an old run down home that was used to cook Meth in just around the corner from her parent's house. Their mother called the ambulance while their Father held what was left of his youngest girl in his arms. Nancy comforted her mother, and it was a long night at the hospital. Marcy's cell phone rung, it was about 10pm and Marcy had decided to stay with Teresa at Nancy's place until they were able to get in contact with her. Nancy was crying uncontrollably."

"Hello," Marcy answered.

"My little sister was shot and killed tonight," Nancy said while crying uncontrollably.

"My God where are you?" Marcy shouted.

"I'm in New Brunswick, just 30 miles east of us, I never told you but that's where my parents live."

Marcy muffled the phone to let Teresa know that Nancy's little sister had been killed.

"We're on our way, what hospital are you at?"

"New Brunswick Memorial." While the sighs and moans continued from their best friend.

Marcy and Teresa were there with their best friend and her parents, within 45 minutes. Marcy and Teresa wrapped their arms around Teresa and held her there. When the paper work was complete the family was told that they could go home and get some rest. Marcy and Teresa along with Nancy's Mom and Dad went home. Marcy followed Nancy's parents to their house, which was a 15 minute drive from the hospital. Nancy road with her parents. Marcy and Teresa took the room that Nancy grew up in and Nancy took the living room couch. Mr. Taylor's face was as stone, from the shock of seeing his baby girl like that, he was covered in his daughters blood, and after hours of tears and shock, he fell asleep with his wife in his arms.

They all awoke the next morning with Marcy giving her immediate supervisor a call letting her know that she and Teresa would not be in to work, because of the death of a relative. Nancy also called her workplace at the warehouse. They all sat to the table for waffles, bacon and orange juice.

The mood was tranquil, then Nancy's mother spoke'

"We really appreciate this Teresa and Marcy, thank you for being here, I know that this is a very bad time for meeting you both, but this is it, these drugs are taking all of our young people, we either have to go visit them in jail or the graveyard, it's sad." Mrs. Taylor lamented.

Meanwhile it was evening and Tonya had secured everything at home with her daughter Tracy. They were all sitting inside Tonya's living room watching TV, Tonya and Pete were sitting close to each other and Tracy and her little brother Mack were across the room on the huge sectional sofa, then Tonya spoke.

"You alright, baby?" Tonya asked Tracy.

"Yes ma'am."

Tracy got out of her position on the sofa, and went and snuggled up under her mother's arms. Tracy's suspension was over and she was due to return to school the next day. Tonya put her arms around her daughter then asked.

"You got your clothes and everything ready for school tomorrow."

"Yes ma'am." Tracy said very humbly and respectfully.

Pete smiled rather cavalier and proud seeing that Tonya was in so much control after catching her teen daughter in bed with a nineteen year old young man.

"Baby, I'm really proud of the way you handled that situation," Pete said.

Tonya kissed Pete and told the kids to go upstairs and get ready for the next school day. While the kids were upstairs getting themselves ready for the next day, Pete kissed Tonya again along with feeling between her thick thighs.

"Damn!", responded Tonya, as she opened up her thighs a little wider so that he'll have access to her succulent womanhood, which was now wet.

"I just need to smell it baby, you know you always smell like fresh sex, acknowledged Pete, as he massaged the wetness between her legs. Pete licked his fingers while Tonya looked at him and told him,

"It's more where that came from and you can have all you want". Tonya stated as she got up and switched off the TV and grabbed Pete by the hand and led him to her upstairs bedroom. As she passed each of her kids' room she told them good night and for each of them to say their prayers before they hit the bed. Tonya and Pete entered her dark, chilled room and closed the door, no words were said Pete placed Tonya on one of the front corners of the bed, held her thighs apart in a mid buck position, and started consuming her pussy. Pete had already swallowed a Libigrow (a sexual stimulant that works better than Viagra) and ate a pint of raw shucked oysters earlier, so his swipe was harder than an African diamond. They laid and made love and cooled out until dawn. As the sun was rising and cool air was blowing through the vents in the room. Tonya put one leg around Pete and said."

"Thank you baby,"

She was appreciating the advice he'd given her on dealing with her daughter.

Pete turned to her and said.

"Baby, do you know that 5000 women are killed each year for something they did that was immoral or against the laws in their country. Women and young girls; just recently over in the middle east, a father paraded the head of his daughter around the city because she dated and had sex with a guy that the father didn't approve of, the guy was of another religion or something... can you believe that?" He continued ... "Decapitated his daughters head and carried her head around the city, because she so called crippled his honor, isn't that sad?"

"Damn, shit that's sick", was Tonya's response

"Well, I need to head for the office early we have a big case we're working on." Pete stated.

"Well, call me at my office at the school anytime baby," Tonya said.

Pete looked at her and took both her breast in his mouth.

"I must've come about eight times last night; I'm hoping I'll be able to walk." Tonya stated.

Pete hopped out of bed and slid on his trousers, shirt, socks and shoes and headed out of the house. He had a key to the house so he locked the door behind him. The children were to be up and out of the house in an hour. Tonya usually leaves before each of them. She grabbed her cell phone and called in to the administration's mailbox letting the secretary know that she would be in late. Tonya laid in her bed and enjoyed the silence; she is giving her children the opportunity to be totally responsible, no words from mom.

An hour had passed and her son peeped through the door and said, love you ma, then left the house. Soon afterwards Tracy knocked on her mother's door, dressed like a traditional fifteen year old, with books in her back pack the whole nine, she opened her mother's door and said."

"I really love you momma, and I'll try to never hurt you again."

Tonya just stared at her daughter, then after a long pause she smiled and said,

"C'mere baby"… Tonya had her arms spread as they embraced tightly.

"Love you." Then kissed her daughter on the cheek. "Uumm, huumm, have a good one baby see ya'll this evening." Tonya whispered.

Tracy grabbed her book bag and headed out of the door. All of her girlfriends were waiting in their usual spot after first period, the senior hall before you get to the cafeteria. Even though Tracy was only a ninth grader, she hangs with nothing but older girls. Everyone in Tracy's crew had reps for breaking some type of school rule, or rules period, they didn't care and was surly on their way to failing in life for sure. When the second period bell had wrong, Tracy went straight to her second period class. She no longer wanted to be labeled a 'Bad Girl'. One of the main reasons for Tracy's new attitude was her mother Tonya. Tracy knew for whatever reason she had escaped with her life, and was sold out on not getting on her mother's bad side again.

Her day was different and was going well, one of her good friends, who is in her third period class and hangs with the girls asked Tracy what happened to her during the first and second period break between classes.

"Girl I'm good, but I think I'm gonna start changing some things in my life right now, my mother had a long talk with me last night. I really feel that I'd like to go to college, and the way I was going that wasn't going to happen. Basically Sonia, I just don't want to end up like some of these girls I see in this city you know, no high school education, two or three kids and on welfare or some government assisted program without the dad being there."

Her friend paused and looked at Tracy with admiration and said.

"Damn, all of that you said...I think I'm going to start changing some things in my life, that shit is real what you just said. I'll let the others know that you're on the path. Damn I've got my senior year coming up and I really got to buckle down in my classes, man fuck all of that bullshit we've been doing...I got to get it. I'll be eighteen next year I really got to get my shit together." Sonia said quickly.

Pete called Tonya at 12 and told her that he wouldn't be picking her up for lunch.

"Hello".

"Yeah baby it's me... I won't be picking you up for lunch today. We're in a case where a cop shot this sixteen year old kid in the back. I'm representing the kid, the cop's excuse was that the kid had a weapon and he didn't. We're looking into suing the police department and the city. Hey baby, I should be there about 5 tonight, I'll bring Chinese."

"Alright baby that sounds good, I'll buy the drinks and I'll get you a 5th of Hen so you can relax even though I know you're trying to stop drinking."

"Yes I am."

"Well, it'll be here."

"Alright then, I'll be there tonight, good-bye."

"Good bye… Love you baby, kiss." Tonya said as she hung up the phone.

School was out and Tracy had just gotten off of the school bus and was a block away from the house, she saw her little brother Mack and waited for him to catch up with her.

"How was your day?" Tracy asked.

"It was alright, these dudes wanted me to skip class and go to the laundry mat around the corner from the school and put fake dollar bills into the coin machine, dollar bills and fives that they printed up off a computer." Mack said.

"What did you do?" Tracy asked.

"You know what I did…you got away with murder. You know I won't even try Momma like that…after she gave you a break, I wasn't about to feel the wrath."

Tracy laughed at her little brother as they turned the key and entered the house. Mack went upstairs and started doing his homework; Tracy checked the messages that were on the machine. She got the message that they were having Chinese, so she sat the dishes out the dining room table and heated water in the kettle to make fresh iced tea; afterwards she sat on the couch and started studying.

Nancy, Marcy and Teresa were attending the funeral, the Pastor spoke from the pulpit.

"I'm hoping that this will stop in our little community, the dope, the crack, the Methamphetamines, the damn Oxycotins…excuse my language yawl. This is the third funeral this month, dealing with some type of drug. I urge the police department to start kicking down some doors in every neighborhood where they expect illegal drug activity." The Pastor lamented.

After the funeral, Marcy walked over to the pastor and handed him the number of Mr. Norton Kay. Mr. Taylor and his wife's family were there from different areas of the map; all were shocked and sadden that a young lady who was just starting life had gotten struck down like that.

Soon afterwards, Marcy and Teresa helped Mrs. Taylor with the clean up and they sat and kept her company into the night. The ladies had the car packed, and Nancy caught a ride back with Marcy and Teresa. On their way back to the city the topic was about struggle and what effects it will have on an individual if they shrug away from it. Marcy spoke.

"That's what this life is about struggle, it's a struggle for a mother to give birth to child, it hurts, but after the struggle then there is ease." Teresa added on.

"The hard times we faced when we all were going through it, with crack. I can remember not having a dime the next morning after I had spent a thousand dollars the night before, then 8am the next morning I won't have a dime. The next week did the same exact thing after I'd gotten paid. I was addicted to murder and couldn't figure out how to stop killing myself. Yeah we all know that it's a struggle but then comes ease when we put those things down that damage us."

"I agree." Nancy replied. They can talk about the economy all they want, if we don't have one thing that will put everything back together and that's simple cooperation and togetherness, this nation will continue to fall. The number one reason why the Japanese, Chinese and Great Brittan progress so is because they have cooperation. The generation of the 40's, 50's, 60's and 70's had one thing, cooperation. The selfishness and me attitude will continue to be the fall of this nation. I don't care anything about the genius scientist they have, if you can't get these scientist to live and work together in harmony, they'll never get a thing done."

As they were pulling into the city Marcy spoke.

"I could remember when I was smoking dope, anything and everything would make me go get a hit. Soon I started making bad shit happen, just so that I'll have a reason to smoke."

"You know all of us have been there, doing five years locked up when I had all the freedom in the world. I'm not on anyone's plantation, I don't have to go to the back of a restaurant to eat, or go thirty miles away to get a hotel room when there is one around the corner from my house. Yes I have learned to thank God daily, simply because I have basic freedom." Teresa stated.

Marcy had requested a week off from work, Teresa did the same and even though Teresa and Nancy are roommates, they really needed the personal time together.

Marcy spent the night over at Nancy's and Teresa's, the lady's showered and like teens at a slumber party, they were walking around in pajamas, popping popcorn, making smoothies and watching the latest bootlegged movies. The ladies gathered on a comforter on the floor in front of the Big screen T.V...

"Nancy what's the latest on your man, damn he's been in there for awhile."

Nancy gave Marcy a rather sagacious look and said.

"Shit I don't know, that's out of my mind. It's ya'll girl. I aint gone lie, I appreciate ya'll, God is real… I got him in my life and I've got ya'll. Just when I was about to go back to smoking that shit, God sent you Marcy to step in and he got rid of that distraction for me. Aint no telling where I'd be. The ladies were cooling, just feeling good about life and each other.

"Girl you know who I feel like seeing or talking to."

"Who?" Teresa asked.

"Judy and Tonya."

"Oh shit, you called one out then damn. I would like to know if they're alright. Ya'll know they let Judy go from that shit we got into… with that dude Fred and his check shceme; I heard he's on his death bed for having that Package (AIDS). Judy only got probation and a couple of months from that absurdity, I caught 6 years, so she should be around here somewhere. Ya'll remember we got that girl to smoking, Nan you remember that first night?" Teresa stated.

"Shit, how can I forget it, the bitch tried to kill me then I hooked up with that nigga Skip and he really tried to kill me. Marcy cased him up though. While you and Judy were doing ya'll thing I was trying to dip and dab in that madness, and almost lost my life fucking with that crack?" Nancy stated very plainly.

"Y'all just seemed to have forgotten what we've learned in those NA meetings. Don't talk too much about those war stories and of all of our conditions, study the present; and clean away from all of that bullshit. Yeah, I know its therapeutic talking about all of our using days, I get down like that myself, but for some reason in my heart, I feel like none of that past shit is going to do us no good." Marcy adamantly said.

"Damn, what are we doing? We're supposed to be enjoying each other and sleeping with Daphne in our hearts," Teresa added.

All three of the ladies agreed.

They played a couple games of Tunk, and called it sleep soon afterwards. They awoken the next morning and had breakfast at a local waffle house. The morning was beautiful out and the ladies were light conversing with each other. After they finished they're breakfast they headed to the mall. They shopped around for awhile until they worked up a hunger. Nancy, Teresa ordered Pizza at the Orange Tree while Marcy ordered two chili dogs and a personal pizza. They took seats a table in the food court and Teresa was having concerns about her longtime friend landing that job with school board as they ate there lunch.

"Nan listen to me you're going to get that job." Teresa expressed to her friend.

Nancy just watch all of the young people moving around up and down the mall, some we're going to the movie theatre, some you could tell were young lovers and just holding hands walking in the cool lustrous mall, taking in all of the benefits of being young, healthy and free. Marcy was entirely engulfed, and dedicated to eating her pizza from the orange tree. She watched her friends while taking a huge bite out of a slice.

"I'm going to type you a letter. It may be some exaggerating in it, but you're going to get that job. So many of us are denied an opportunity for a job or good career, because of our background. If you suffered for the crime wouldn't that make you a more worthy candidate. Something that you did in your young years comes back to haunt you in your most stable and needful years… that shit aint right." Teresa strongly stated.

Nancy just thought and said.

"There's only one God and that's who I'm depending on."

"That's all you need". Marcy said with pepperoni pizza stuffed in her mouth as she took a sip of the orange slushy.

The ladies did a little shopping and ate ice cream.

"I think I'll call Tonya." Nancy stated as she took out her cell phone from her purse and started dialing the last known number she had of Tonya.

"Hello." Tonya answered, in a mature huskily voice.

"Tonya this is me, Nancy."

"Nancy, Nancy who?"

"Nancy Taylor"

"Girl you gotta be joking."

"What's happening?" Nancy asked.

"Nancy, it's so nice to hear your voice, God is good isn't he?"

"All the time and every time." Nancy responded.

"Hey Nan, I'm getting married and I'd like for you to come…give me your address and I'll send you an invitation, it should be about 5 months from now, but we'll be in contact before then. Is this the number where you can be reached?"

"Yes." Nancy said.

"Well I'll call you tonight from the house I'm sort of trying to get these kids on the up and up at this school, I'm an assistant principal here in Atlanta." She continued. "Damn, do they even have any parents like we had anymore? You can't walk in my house and at 11 years of age and be in the 4th grade. And they blame us in the school system for the product we produce…if you take a shit I can't wipe your ass for you. And when they don't work with these children when they get home, cut the TV off, no video games just books, pencils and paper. It's not hard, these parents need to visit these schools, talk to the child's teacher and have their asses to the neck in Math, Reading, Science and more until the summer comes, that's how we did it , didn't we?"

"Yeah, it made the summer that much better, knowing that you're not behind, but shit we had mamas who didn't play that shit, all they want to do these days is buy the kid this, give the kid that instead of giving them something that's going to carry them for the rest of their lives and that's having them to acquire knowledge and education. Nancy stated as she gave Tonya her address. As Nancy and Tonya continued to chat the ladies went from inside of the mall into the mall's parking lot… to go home.

"Damn, who was that Michelle Obama?" Marcy asked, sharp-witted as she usually is.

"Teresa, you remember Tonya." Nancy asked.

"Yeah, what is she up to?"

"Nice home in Atlanta, getting married, an assistant principal at a high school, and her kids are doing well in school."

"We grow out of it, but the sad part is some don't. Some get out of the crack world as a resort of jail or death." Teresa said reflecting on how Tonya was a huge dope dealer in the game back in the day and changed her life and is benefiting from it.

Marcy dropped Nancy and Teresa off.

"Alright ya'll be nice, I've got to get up and go to work in the morning."

"Alright girl, call us." They said as they went inside of the house.

As soon as they got inside of the house, Teresa went to work on the letter for Nancy in her room on her laptop. Nancy walked to the living room, kicked off her shoes sprawled out on the couch with a pillow under her head and relaxed until she dozed off into a pleasant sleep.

All the while on the other side of town Die was in bed with his lady Sheena, it was about 3 in the morning. They had just finished smoking a fat blunt of weed. Die kept talking about Dale... how he was as a youngster.

"Yeah baby, I couldn't believe how good that nigga was, in everything-sports, drawing, and dressing. The nigga was the style king. He was the man back in the day, but I know he's smoking...I know he is."

"Dale man I'm tired... I really don't want to hear none of that shit right now. Man just shut up Please!" Sheena exclaimed.

Die thought for a second and then erupted.

"Bitch, don't ever in your motherfuckin life tell me to shut-up...you hear me, ever in your life. Bitch, I take care of you, and it aint shit for me to throw your ass out. As a matter of fact, get your shit and get out of my place!" Die exclaimed.

Sheena was tired and high and really didn't feel like doing too much of nothing, let alone having to leave her bed at that time in the morning, it would really be a nightmare, both physically and mentally. She knew Die was serious and tried to pacify his anger.

"Man C'mon, you know I really didn't mean that."

"You got 20 minutes to get out of here."

Sheena got up slow and headed for the closet, and started packing her things in a large duffle bag that layed on the floor in the closet.

Die went to the kitchen and made himself a ham sandwich and poured a glass of orange juice, stepped inside of his living room and sat in his recliner and hit the remote on his TV. Sheena had her duffle bag strapped over her shoulder; she was dressed in a tight blue spandex suit and a white hoody. Sheena opened the door and looked back at Die Boy and said.

"I'll see you soon motherfuckah." As she slammed the door behind her with a smile on her face. Die had no response. Sheena made it down the stairs into the courtyard and looked around, she thought about damaging his car but didn't, instead she walked across the street to the pay phone and dialed a cab. Sheena has no relatives and the only friend she had was Die Boy. The cab arrived in 10minutes. Sheena had always kept money, since she was the girlfriend of the most successful crack dealer in the city. The cabbie pulled in near the pay phone where Sheena stood. The cabbie got out of the cab and put Sheena's bag in the back seat, closed the door and secured himself under the wheel as Sheena fastened her seatbelt on the passenger side.

"Where to, ma'am?"

"Down town…do you know if the mission is taking anyone at this time of the morning?" Sheena asked the Cabby.

"Oh, yes ma'am, especially women and children. I personally know the owner of that mission, and he doesn't play about women and children sleeping on the street, and if he doesn't have room he'll make room, they'll kick out a couple of those male transients…so what's a pretty young lady like you going to the mission for?"

Sheena didn't say a word; she just stared straight ahead, and said.
"Oh, it's nothing, just get me downtown."
"OK pretty lady, downtown it is."
They get into town less than 15 minutes. There also was a choice of missions she could stay at. While driving slowly the Cab Driver stated,

"Ma'am, I'm going to take you to the one my friend owns, it's really the biggest and the cleanest facility of them all."

They pull in front of the mission, Sheena handed the driver a 10 dollar bill, even though the meter read $7.60, and told him to keep the change. She retrieved her bag out of the back seat and the Driver sped off. Sheena had her things and walked down the corridor which led to glass double doors. There was a male Transient who didn't get a bed that night smoking a cigarette outside of the double doors. The gentleman opened the door for Sheena, behind the receptionist desk there awaited two gentlemen who were in the mission's program and greeted Sheena as she walked through the door.

"Yes, may I help you ma'am?"

"Yes, I would like to have a place to stay for a week or two if that's possible?" She asked.

"Do you have children with you ma'am?"

"No."

"Alright, ma'am if you can fill out this card with all of your relevant information on it I'll show you to our women's side of the facility." The receptionist stated.

After she filled out the form, the guy led her to the women's side of the mission.

"OK ma'am, here's your bed, we have wake up at 6am, breakfast ends at 8am, they hand out fresh linen at that compartment over there every day along with feminine products and fresh towels, will there be anything else ma'am?"

"No, and thank you."

"OK, have a good night or what's left of It.", stated the receptionist.

Sheena put her things under her bed and stretched out on the bed and dozed off.

Die- boy was smoking weed watching ESPN. Soon it was time for the ladies to wake-up; they all washed up and headed for the cafeteria. One of the transients there who is a smoker recognized Sheena who was piddling around in her tray, because nothing was fit to eat on it, but she drank the orange juice.

"Sheena… girl what you doing in here?" The middle age lady shouted from across the room. Sheena kept her head down and kept sipping on the orange juice. The lady grabbed her tray and headed for the table where Sheena was sitting. The transient took a seat.

"Damn Sheena what you doing down here?" The lady buys crack from Sheena on the regular.

"Aint nothing, I just got to go do something real fast," Sheena said as she got out of her seat, emptied the tray and head out of the side door of the mission. There was a McDonalds across the street from the mission, she was incredibly hungry so she went in and ordered herself a McGriddle a cup of coffee and a large orange juice. There was USA Today on the table at the booth where she sat, Sheena opened up the paper and started browsing through it, until a press conference of the President of the United States of America Barak Obama caught her attention on the 54inch screen that hanged on the wall. It's been a fantastic past year and half with him as President. He has an 80% approval rating and has every young and old American away from the war. No more deaths are due to the diplomatic aptitude he and the Vise President has a unique gift of. Sitting down to talk and not fight, becoming brothers and sisters for Pease all across the world.

The main part for the high approval rating was because there were no more American deaths due to warring. Even the relations and tension in the Middle East has calmed down… Sheena finished up her breakfast and took a B-Line to the Police Department. Her thoughts were only on revenge. She went through the metal detectors and walked over to the receiving desk.

"Yes ma'am how may I help you", offered the female officer sitting behind the desk.

"I would like to speak with the Sheriff or anyone of authority."

The officer pushed the button on the phone and she said.

"There is a young lady up here that would like to speak with you."

"Have her to come on back." The Sheriff stated.

The receptionist pointed to the office and gave her the number on the door. Sheena took a slow stroll down the corridor; she opened the door to the office and walked in. The Captain told her to have a seat, Sheena did that.

"Oh I apologize I'm Chief Sheriff Jeffery Newsom, how may I help you today?"

"I would like to know if you want to know about a guy that's providing 90% of the dope in this city." Sheena said.

"Yes ma'am I'm very interested in that, who and where is this person?"

"Over on Riverdale, on the west bank of the city."

"How do you know this person?" The Sheriff questioned.

"I use to date him, his name is Steve Bass, everybody knows him as Die-Boy she added. His address is 112 Hampton Street.

The Sheriff had the record button on, as he got the information from Sheena. He told her that he'll get on it and that it would be quick, he also let her know that it would be confidential.

"Thank you Sheriff". Sheena said.

"No… thank you, you know what really gets me about this drug is that the children suffer badly and if I can get crack off of every neighborhood and street in the world, I'll do it." He continued. "The mother buys crack with the grocery money, the light bill and rent or mortgage doesn't get paid, and who does all of this fall onto?"

"The children", Sheena added.

"Exactly!" He added on…

"Imma be real with you ma'am, I'm going to clean this city up as of today. I don't want any innocent kids going through this hell when I can do something about it. 'Sheriff Newsom closed, as Sheena got up and headed for the door, The Sheriff got up and shook her hand as Sheena headed out. She walked down the corridor wave at the receptionist and walked out of the glass doors of the station. Sheriff Newsom got on the phone and called the Mayor.

"Yes sir, how are you today Mayor this is Sheriff Newsom I just wanted you to know that I'll be doing a drug sweep around the city this week, I'm just letting you know so you won't be in the blind."

"Now that's what I'm talking about, we're getting soft, not putting in work. The kids suffer the most, we're going to change all of that, if they don't have any Crack to buy, then they can't smoke it, and the money can go on food to feed their kids and rent or mortgage to provide a descent roof for them." The Mayor stated.

"Bulls eye", was the Sheriff's response.

After he hung up the phone with the Mayor, Newsom notified all of the officers working in that jurisdiction. The announcement of instructions blared through each officer's radio.

"We're going to do a drug bust off of Hampton over there in Riverdale, 112 Hampton street , you guys need to take notes on the activity that's going on over there, stay out eyes view and don't patrol any squad cars in that area. I've got a guy that's coming to make a purchase there today. I need for you guys not to blow this. I really need for you guys to stay out of eyes view of this guy, just park on a neighboring block or something and jot down all the activities, I'll put together a team first thing in the morning so we can get to work, 10-4." All of the officers had gotten the update.

It was 10am and Die was talking with one of the young peddlers, inside of his apartment.

"Nigga this shit is real wit me my nigga, and when I say it… it's just what it mean." Die exclaimed, he continued. "I gave you 3000 dollars worth of dope to sell. All I wanted you to do, was bring me my money. You come up in here huffing and puffing giving me 2500 dollars, where's the rest of my loot nigga?"

"Man, niggas be coming up asking for shorts." The young man responded.

"I don't give a fuck, get mines my nigga and the next time I see you, you better have my 500 dollars. I ought to slap you with this pistol; just dip up out my shit my nigger… for real."

The young man left the apartment feeling dejected but hopeful. His 14 year old sister thought that he created the ground for us to walk on; she admired her older brother that much. He went back to his house where he lives with his mother and 14 year old sister. He didn't have any more of the money, he basically used the extra loot to get his little sister some shoes and a couple of outfits and helped his mother out with groceries and rent, now it was do or die time, he needed a job so, he put his application in to the Youth Advocates of America and got back into high school. He didn't tell anyone anything. He realized that he needed to get Die his money, because he didn't want any unexpected incidents, so he went on a limb and called his uncle who had a business and would do anything for his nephew. But the young man rarely called him. This particular time he was calling his uncle to let him know that he had gotten back in school and had a job …

"Boy how's your mama?" The uncle asked.

"She's alright; she doesn't know that I'm back in school and working."

"Now that's positive, I miss ya'll… tell her that I'm bringing everything that goes into that Gumbo…I need for her to make me a pot this weekend, tell her, alright. And I'm proud of you boy for holding down your mother and sister the way you're doing… like a man and nothing else."

"Preciate it Unc." The young man said to his uncle. He continued… "Man Unk, you know I don't usually ask you for anything…but I need a favor."

"What's that?"

"I need about five-hundred dollars. I'll kick it back to you when I get my check, alright man."

"Nah…you don't have to pay me back nothing…you just stay in school and keep working, that'll be your payback." He continued. "Nephew, for me to suit up and come to your graduation this year, is payback enough. Some'ing like your Grandma use to say…"I want to see you walk"… "Where you at?"

"I'm at the house".

"Well I'll bring that package by to you. Be outside because I'm on a job. So be outside and I 'll be there in about fifteen minutes."

The detectives had Die boy's apartment staked out. There was plenty of activity at Die's apartment all day. It was as if he was the only one in the city that had dope. Die had four Kilos of powder, two Kilo's of cooked crack, and two pounds of marijuana in the back room in the closet of his apartment.

It was one of Die's best days ever since dealing dope. People were getting served three at a time. He had cats coming from the other side of town coming to buy weight, four and five cookies at a time. One of the major players in the game on the other side of town was stating...

"Man, give me six of them three-hundred dollar cookies, I'll probably be back in a couple hours, man aint no dope nowhere." The dealer stated.

The activity was so much that Die Boy had to close up shop. He decided to call up one of his partners, a dude by the name of Fahlo.

"Yo Fahlo man, I need you here, this shit got me more shook than Barney Phyfe, I'm nervous man, I think I'll close up shop." Die said.
"Nah, don't close up shop, give me about ten minutes let me get some of that cheddah, my nigga." Fahlo stated.
"You better hurry up then."
"Alright man, Peace." Fahlo said as he closed his cell phone.

Sheriff Jeffrey Newsom had made contact with one his best detectives.

"Sheriff, what's happening, and when am I going to get on those Links with you? You know the last time we hit the course I smashed you." Detective Bullock expressed.

"Yeah man after we get this project done. I'll catch you back out there and I'm gonna fly that head, aiight. Hey check this out I've got something big for you to get on, ASAP." Newsom said.

Detective Bullock is one of the best undercover agents in the south. He looks like a dealer, smoker, and speaks the language of the gutter streets.

"Spit it." Bullock quickly said.
"Got this cat over there on Riverdale, 112 Hampton Street. He's pumping allot of dope over there, all I want you to do is check him out." The Sheriff stated.
"I'll do that... you got that." Bullock responded.
"Get back with me," the Sheriff offered.

Detective Bullock got suited and booted, and called his main man DT Collins for help.

"Yo, let's go buy some dope." Bullock acknowledged to his partner through his cell phone.

"Yo, you know where I'm at? I'm over at the pool hall on 45th."

Die Boy's partner Fahlo, had arrived at Die's apartment, he knocked on the door.
"Who is it?"
"Fahlo," he answered Die through the door with a deep voice.

Die peeped through the peep hole and let him in. There was a stack of 10's and 20's lying by Die's recliner, about 3000 dollars. Fahlo started to sit in the recliner, Die stopped him.

"Nah man, sit over there. Nigga I know all of you 'Johnny Slick' mua-fuchahs." Die stated.
"Ah nigga, go to hell with that shit, man." Fahlo responded, as he took his place on the sofa and fired up a Newport. There was another knock on the door.

"Yeah?"
"Hey Die man, this me, Pip".
Die let him in.
"Need 6 of them…50 dollar slabs." Pip stated.

Die stepped inside the dining area, got 6 slabs out of the China cabinet and placed them in Pip's hand.

"Man aint no dope in this city, aint nobody got none. I went over there on the south side of town to get some dope from Block and them, guess what?"

"What?" Die asked.
"Nothing! Them niggas talking bout coming over here to get some dope from you." Pip said.
"Man I might close up, in about an hour or two." Die said. Letting Pip out of the door as he took his money.

D etective Bullock picked his partner, DT Collins up from the pool hall
on 45th and Moncrief in a '72 hooptie. They get over to Riverdale a
block away from Die's apartment.

"I need to catch a chick out here geeking, who knows this nigga
Die, so she can get familiar with me, know what I'm saying." Detective
Bullock offered.

"Yeah I'm looking, yo there she is right there." Collins said.

There was a young woman pacing back and forth in front of the
convenience store looking like she needed it a bump of dope bad. They
pulled up next to her.
"Yo baby, where can I get some hard from around here." Bullock
asked.

The young lady rushed to the car, and started to get into the back
seat.
"Hold up baby, before you get in here." Collins shouted.
The lady was desperate and started capping on Collins.

"Man fuck you, I aint got time for this shit, she said as she started
to walk away."
"Yo, he's with me sweetheart and I apologize. Get in baby. Who is
it and where do we have to go?" Bullock asked.
She hopped into the backseat and closed the door.

"This nigga name Die, he serves right up in those apartments right there, that nigga got the best crack in this motherfuckah… for real." She stated.

They pulled in front of Die's apartment. She gets out of the backseat and walks to Detective Bullock side.

"So what ya'll wanna get, that nigga got pies, cookies, slabs, quarters, whatever you want… dimes, twenties."

"Yo baby slow down, I need about fifty for now you aint gonna run off wit my money and shit are you… can I go up there with you?" Bullock asked.

"Look here nigga, I smoke dope, I don't play these games and shit, and hell no you can't come up here with me." Stated the young lady.

Detective Bullock handed her a fifty dollar bill, while putting his revolver on the dash board. She saw the revolver and her entire attitude changed to respect after she saw the gun.

"Hey man I'll bring you back your dope, but you aint getting nothing if you come up there with me."

"What's your name?" Bullock asked.

"They call me 'Starchy Cat.' She answered as she strolled off to go cop the crack. Detective Bullock was only thinking about knocking Die Boy's door off the hinges. Bullock cut the car off and he and Collins waited. They saw the building she went in and soon they'll learn more. She came back and got into the back seat of the vehicle and handed Detective Bullock five rocks. He didn't say anything, instead he handed Starchy Cat two of the rocks without breaking one. She hadn't seen that much graciousness since she started smoking ten years ago. He would've given her all of it but he didn't want to blow his cover.

"Damn man, I really appreciate this, ya'll get high?…I got a lil piece of stem on me."

"Nah baby we're going to move on, but I'd like to get another package in an hour from now." Bullock said.

Cat knew the potency of Die-Boy's crack and knew that it would take an hour to smoke the rocks. Die cooks and sell crack not for money but for the smoker to enjoy.

"I'll be in that same spot, just be there to get me."

"Hey I need to go up there with you and cop the next time."

"We'll talk about that when the time comes, I'll see ya'll, I got to go." Cat stated.

Bullock and Collins drove off and Cat went to her Cat Hole, her designated place to smoke at. On her way to the Cat Hole which was a block away from Hampton Street, from where Die lives, she spots a friend Vanessa who was sitting on the porch smoking a Newport. Vanessa lives with Will, a sixty -six year old retired mechanic. He lives in an old shot gun house, that looks like it's about to fall apart.

"What's up girl," Vanessa stated.

Cat signaled for her to come to the Cat Hole with her. Vanessa leaves the porch and walks with Cat to the Cat Hole. Starchy Cat opened her hand and Vanessa saw the two dime rocks. She didn't say anything, because she knows that Cat does not like to talk much or have anyone around her that runs their mouth while she's getting high. They get to the hole and Cat sits in an old office chair while Vanessa sits on an old stool. Starchy Cat broke one of the dimes in half and handed it to Vanessa.

Vanessa waited for Cat to mount up. Cat retrieved a nearly new glass stem she had hidden from under some leaves. She put the full dime away and melted the half of dime piece on top of the stem. She took her lighter out of her pocket and blasted. Vanessa immediately followed and pulled off of her stem. Cat sat the stem and lighter down and started looking around her and on the ground as if she dropped a piece. Vanessa was smooth sitting in one spot, exhaling the crack smoke out of her nose slowly. The dope was fire, Vanessa wanted to say something badly, but didn't. A bit of spittle excreted from the corners of her mouth, but she was silent as Cat situated herself in her seat. Starchy Cat broke Vanessa off another piece and handed it to her.

Vanessa put the piece on top of the stem, melted it then took a twig from the ground, and pushed the packed stem, then lit it. She inhaled an even more powerful stream of smoke. Cat put the remaining piece on her stem and hit it; she sat still this time, but said something. She was still staggered from the toxic influence of the crack she had just smoked. She said in a low, quiet tone of voice.

"I got two dudes who are supposed to pick me up in a few minutes."

"Oh yeah?" Vanessa stated.

Yeah, I'm gonna get up and make a move, because you know I'll get stuck if I sit here, so I'd better force myself to get up, give me a Newport." Vanessa gave her a Port. Cat lit the Newport and got up and started walking out of the cat hole. Vanessa followed and as they walked side by side.

"Cat we're are about to come up to the house, I'm going in there and get you a shot of liquor and couple of Newports so you could handle your business." They get to old man Will's house and Vanessa rushed into the screen door and Cat sat on the front porch. She went to the back of the old wooded Shot gun house and went in old man Will's room where he was sprawled out on his bed watching television. Vanessa went to his liquor table and attempted to pour Cat a drink of Jim Bean.
"What in the fuck you think you doing girl?!" Old man Will asked.
"Oh...Will, I'm going to pour my friend a drink, she needs it bad." Vanessa explained.
"Shiiit, you know I don't play that shit wit a motherfuckah... fucking wit my liquor!" Will blasted.

"That's Starchy Cat out there; she said she'll pay ya when she get's something in about thirty minutes."

"Get what? You know damn well I don't smoke that shit, and that's all that lil fine ass motherfuckah does is smoke crack, I don't want no damn crack!" Will strongly stated.

"Nah baby, she's gonna have some money in a bit and she'll straighten you…I'll make sure of that." Vanessa stated.

Will looked at Vanessa and said.

"Go ahead then."

Vanessa took the glass of liquor out to Starchy Cat. Cat needed the drink because she was too geeked. She placed the empty glass back into the hands of Vanessa after she'd gulped down the strong drink, then she lit a Newport. The edge was off of her. She was able to carry on a cool conversation now…without being so paranoid, the kind of paranoid that she'd think someone was coming to chop her head off with a hatchet.

"See I told you that that shit would bring you back, it's about that time for you to handle that… aint it girl?"

Starchy Cat didn't answer; she just looked out into the street as the cars passed by.

"You know where I'm at. The Old man said if you throw him bout twenty dollars Cat nodded in aggreeance and headed off of the porch to handle her business with Detective Bullock and Collins.

Cat left the porch and headed up to the corner store. Detective Bullock and Collins were parked in an undisclosed location and saw Cat as soon as she hit the block. She waited and looked around and tried to spot them. Cat didn't see them, but they saw her and decided to pick her up. They pulled up next to the curb where she stood; Cat got in the backseat.

"You ready?" Bullock asked.

"Yeah". Cat stated.

They pulled up in front of the apartment.

"Hey Yo, I need ten of them, and I want to meet him, I'm hoping you can work this out." Bullock stated.

"That nigga don't wanna meet nobody and if you come up there wanting to buy dope and he don't know you, you might get shot." Cat expressed.

"Yeah baby I feel you on that, get me 10 of them. Tell him that I'd like to get some weight." He continued. "I want you to arrange this and if it's cool for us to meet with him… you wouldn't have to worry about smoking for awhile. Cat, I'll supply you with all of the dope you can smoke." Bullock stated as he gave her the hundred dollar bill."

Cat got out of the car and headed up to Die-Boy's apartment. She knocked on the door and there was a heavy marijuana scent that permeated through the door and out into the hall way.

"Who is it?" Die asked as he peeped through the peep hole, saw that it was Cat and let her in, then closed the door behind her.

"Let me get ten." She stated as she handed him the hundred dollar bill. Die passed the bill to Fahlo, as he told Fahlo to go into the dining room cabinet and get ten dimes out of it, as Fahlo was getting the dope out of the cabinet, Starchy Cat looked at Die and said.

"Man I need to talk with you for real."
"What's happening baby?"

"Man it's this dude that wants to buy some weight from you. I've told him that you don't sell dope to no one you don't know. But I've checked him out he's cool."

"Oh yeah…how do you know he's cool, cause he's buying you dope?" Die boy asked.
"Nah straight up, the nigga alright."
"Girl get out my mothefuckin face with that bullshit…you keep coming to me with this Hansel and Gretel shit… you gonna end up getting dope from somewhere else."
Starchy Cat looked a little dismayed; all she wanted were the drugs that Bullock was supplying her. She really didn't give a fuck about either one of them, Die or Bullock.
"So what do you want me to tell this nigga?" She asked.
"Man, I don't give a fuck what you tell the nigga…give me that dope back… girl you act like you the motherfuckin police."

Starchy Cat left the apartment and headed down the stairs. She got inside of the car and handed Die the 10 rocks. Die gave her 6 of the rocks and fifty dollars.

"So what did he say about me meeting him?" Bullock asked.
"I don't think he's going to do it."
"What happened?" Asked Bullock.
"I think he thinks you're the police."

Out of nowhere a baser started beating the window on Collin's side of the car. Collins let the window down a little.

"Yo man get away from the window!" Collins exclaimed rather authoritatively.
"Give me a piece of dope nigga," ask the baser, who's smoked so much good crack for so long, it made him make sudden involuntary movements, rather unorthodox movements. The cocaine had infected his entire nervous system. The smoker kept clinching his teeth, and jerking his neck, uncontrollably. Collins snatched the gun that was underneath his seat got out of the car and put the gun to the strangers head.

"Nigga, get the fuck away from here...I've already told you I don't have no crack on me nigga!" Collins exclaimed.
"Man crank up the car, that's Peety Roll… ya boy will have to kill that motherfucker. He won't leave till ya'll give him a piece of that dope."
Starchy Cat got out the car, got between Peety Roll and Collins.
"Here nigga", she gave him one of her rocks.
"Now haul ass!" She said as she pushed Collins away from Peety. Peety Roll took the slug of dope, took a couple of steps away and mounted up the slug of crack and hit it.

Cat walked back to the car and signaled for Collins to c'mon. Collins got in the front seat and Cat closed her door in the back. She told detective Bullock,

"Man speed off, because when that nigga come off of that Blast, he'll bust every window out of this car." Cat instructed them.

Bullock drove off around the corner and Starchy Cat told him to park in front of Vanessa's house because that's where she'll be getting off at. Bullock parked and gave Cat fifty dollars and the rest of the dope.

"Man I appreciate this. If y'all need something else I'll be here," Cat stated as she got out of the backseat and closed the door. She was walking up the steps to where Vanessa was sitting on the porch. Bullock let his window down and shouted out of the window.

"Hey baby, thanks, I'll see you later," Cat waived to both of them good-bye.

"Man let me call Newsom, and tell him we can move on this nigga tonight." Die stated.

Yo man, niggas seem like they don't give a fuck about pumping that shit in our neighborhood s, shit niggas already aint got shit as it is and one nigga got all the money while the rest of the community is doing bad, that's fuck up." Collin's expressed.

"Yeah but that's why we're here to get rid of them motherfuckuhs, I don't have no sympathy when we knock down those parasites' doors. I have a deep down repugnance for them leeches. My momma told me long time ago, before she passed she said, Baby if God took twelve to shake up the world, imagine how much he can do with millions on his side. I never forgot that."

Detective Bullock gets in contact with Sheriff Newsom, as he and Collins are heading to a local deli for a sandwich.

"Sheriff, how are you, this Bullock."
"Yeah man what you got?" The sheriff asked.
"We can move on this clown tonight if you want to." Bullock announced.
"Alright then let me get all of these other officers on it and I'll have all of your man power, guns, Kevlar bulletproof vest the whole nine." The Sheriff stated.

"Alright, we'll be down there as soon as I down this sandwich." Bullock said.

"Cool." Sheriff Newsom said as he hung up the phone.

After Bullock and Collins finished their sandwiches they head to the Police Station. Bullock pulls out his cell phone and calls Newsom as they enter the station.

"Hello."

"Yeah man, where are you? We're in the station." Bullock pronounced.

"I'm down in the 'War Room'." Newsom stated.

The 'War Room' is equipped of chalk boards, lockers for the officers and about 30 desks for briefings. Bullock and Collins get deep inside the police station and walk down a long downhill corridor that leads to the War Room, Bullock and Collins walk in the room.

"Bullock what's happening, boy you ready?" Newsom asked.

"Yeah," Bullock answered, as he and Collins walked over to the Sheriff and shook hands.

"Man I got all of those boys over there, ready. Four cop cars and eight men to man those cars. Here are your Kevlar bullet proof vest and some extra ammo, ya'll call me when you got him handcuffed."

Bullock and Collins left the police station and got into their vehicle. Bullock turned on the ignition, looked at Collins and said,

"Let's put it on'em,"

They drove off and headed over to Riverdale.

tarchy Cat and Vanessa are sitting in the old man Will's wooden shot
house. The old man was in his room watching the Nightly News.
Starchy Cat laid all of the dope and money on the table.

"Give me twenty of those dollars and I'll take it back there to him
and you'll be able to smoke your shit in a safe place."

Cat gave Vanessa a twenty dollar bill, and Vanessa took the bill back to
Will and let him know that Starchy Cat was in the living room smoking,
and that she was going to the store. Old man Will always felt an attraction
for Starchy Cat, but knew that she is Vanessa's friend and just really
couldn't catch her right, if he ever had a chance he would try. Vanessa
left the house and went to the store. Starchy Cat took a piece of crack and
mounted it up, she fired it up and took a blast so big and stimulating she
came in her tight shorts that fitted around her Thick thighs, ass and hips
which mounted up into her Mound of Venus. The potency of the dope
reaches to the room where Will was laying in the bed.

"God damn, that little fine bitch up there smoking that shit," Will
said to himself as he put on his robe and poured himself a drink. He
left the room and went up front where Cat was sitting on the couch
with her thighs open; you could see the dampness between her thighs
that seeped through her panties to the shorts that she wore. Will saw
this and knew that she was high, he sat next to her and put his hand on
her thigh. Cat spreaded her thighs further apart, as Will could feel the
dampness between her legs.

Starchy Cat couldn't speak instead her actions told him what she was after; Starchy Cat wanted Will to hit the stem. She didn't care what it took. She was tired of him showing daily, that he was far superior to her and Vanessa, all because they smoked crack and he didn't. She started rubbing on her pussy and taking the buttons loose on her shorts, all while melting a dime on the stem. Cat put one of her hands between Will's robe and started massaging his semi-erection. The only thing that chimed in the old man's head was that he wanted to throw his head between her legs and eat her pussy. Will was gone buy now and his defenses were down. Cat went down and circled around the tip of his erection with her tongue. She sat up then put the stem to his mouth and told him to inhale as she lit the tip of the stem. Will inhaled. She told him to hold the smoke in and slowly exhale out of his nose. He did that as she went down on him and covered his penis with her entire mouth, making spittle and sucking noise as a female fallacious specialist would do.

Will was gone. The ecstasy of the head and fire of the crack brought down Will's entire superior attitude he'd shown towards those that have the illness of crack addiction. From that one taste of pleasure he would succumb to a life that would soon become an unneeded struggle. Cat brought her head up and mounted up a piece for herself and hit it. She put the lighter and stem down, put a hand to the back of Will's head and brought his head between her legs. He was in heaven.

After he orally stimulated her, they both sat up on the sofa. Cat put her shorts back on and Will tied his robe. They traded the stem back and forth as Vanessa walked through the door. Vanessa knew Cat had initiated Will to the stem, by watching the way he was ghosting and fiending. Vanessa sat down in the recliner in front of the coffee table. Now all three of them was gathered around the coffee table as Vanessa emptied the contents in the bag. She handed Cat her orange juice, and put the cigarettes in the center of the table which Cat got one of them out of the box and lit it, then handed Vanessa a block of dope. Vanessa pulled out a fresh glass stem she had in her pocket and took a blast, then put the glass and lighter on the table and started staring at Will as if to say...

"OK motherfuckah, I got yo ass nigh."

Detective Bullock and Collins get to Riverdale and park at a nearby Krispy Kream parking lot. Sheriff Newsom signaled every officer to meet in that nearby parking lot. All the personnel that are part of the bust were filed in the parking lot.

Some of the fellows hadn't seen each other in while and did there 'hey man how you doings', hugs, daps and salutations. Bullock gave the guys a small prep talk and made sure that every man would be in place, when he and Collins move on the apartment.

"Look here, we're getting this motherfucker today, we have to get this one." He stated and continued, "I want you three on the back of the apartment for the desperate dash if somebody jumps out of the window. And Collins and I will take the front." He continued, "You, my man, back me and Collins up, if you see anyone attempting to try us, take their ass out. I want you two at the front of the apartment, ground level. When ya'll hear that door go down come up and help alright, let's get locked and loaded and split this nigga's shit!" Bullock emphatically stated.

All of the fellows took their positions around the apartment. Collins and Bullock hit the staircase and proceeded to go up to Die-Boy's apartment.

"OH BITCH ASS NIGGA, I HAD TO KILL; ALL THEY SEE IS YA PICTURE AT THE FUNERAL." Pulsated from Die's stereo system out into hall. Bullock looked at Collins and said.

"Sounds like he's in there."

"Nah, don't take no chances, just knock one time." He continued. "We can't afford to blow this one." Collins said.

Bullock knocked and Die-Boy turned the music down. That's when Collins bolted the battering Ram full force through the door. Fahlo headed for the back window and jumped from three stories up. Bullock grabbed Die and wrestled him to the ground with the tenaciousness of a pit bull.

Sheriff Newsom arrived to the apartment soon after Die-Boy was handcuffed and read his rights. Fahlo was brought to the front of the apartments. The authorities had to call the Emergency Medical Services, because Fahlo's left leg was broken for his desperate jump from the five story building.

Newsom went up to the apartment and saw all of the wreckage and Evidence Techs were clearing huge amounts of cocaine, crack, money and marijuana from the apartment. Sheriff Newsom started reflecting heavily on Malcolm X, because he knew in heart that if Malcolm was here any man regardless of color in America would be on their way to something substantial, instead of killing each other and or doing huge time for selling any type of petty drug. Bullock walked in the door and heard Newsom reflecting aloud.

"Whoever killed him or whoever had something to do with his death. No matter how much they shine or impress chumps on this planet; whoever had something to do with his death will live their next consciousness and existence in pure hell."

"What are you talking about Sheriff?" Bullock asked.

"Oh, nothing man, I was just reflecting on something. Just reflecting on why we've taken this turn in the maze, crack addiction, murdering each other, early pregnancy and abuse of our homes and lives; we've just taken the turn to hell. Just thinking about if brother Malcolm was alive, how farther along in the game we'd be. My mother left me with something to keep me though. She said, "If he took twelve, just think of what he'll do with millions on his side." Newsom reflected.

"We got two of them cuffed and in the back of the car, ready to be booked." Bullock stated.

"Fine, take'em down there. What is that?" The Sheriff asked one of the Evidence Technicians.

"It's crack Sir."

"Crack?" Let me see that."

It was a brief case full of cookies and slabs; all individually wrapped in cellophane and band with rubber bands.

"Man looks like we've taken two out the game, now it's time to get the ones who bring this bullshit over here."

"Yeah, that's going to be the real task." Bullock stated as he and Sheriff Newsom walked out of the apartment.

Tonya and her fiancé Pete were having dinner along with Tonya's two kids Mack and Tracy. They'd made plans to get married. Pete started Tonya to having dinner with her kids, it aimed at getting the children in the habit of sharing their day to day activities with her, regardless if their day was good or bad. Tracy, her daughter; grades had improved tremendously along with the great attitude she now possessed. And Tonya's son Mack continued to have an innate ability of making good decision at a young age. Pete's law firm has him on the case of a young man that was shot down by the city's police. He's representing the mother of the slain youth.

"So how's the case going baby?" Tonya asked.

"Well it turned out that the young man that was killed had a water gun on him. The officer patted him down while having secured one handcuff on his wrist. The officer felt the gun in his jacket. The young man took off running, with jacket in the officer's hand. He got about twenty yards separation from the officer, that's when the cop shot him four times…all four above the waist." Pete expounded.

"Damn, that's worth suing for." Tonya expressed.
"I've heard word through the grapevine that the city is going to try and settle out of court with her for two million." Pete said.
"That's great, I'm tired of these officers shooting our kids, just killing them," She lamented.
"You would think from all of that training they get, they'll be able

to shoot for a spot that would injure instead of kill, and that was our primary argument." Pete said.

"No amount of money is worth the life of your child, but we can't let them kill off our youth. I constantly tell those two up there, that if they're out there violating in any kind of way, the system got a place to put'em and it want be pretty." Tonya strongly expressed.

They cleaned the dishes off of the table. Tracy and Mack went upstairs to get ready for the next school day. Pete and Tonya moved to the comfortable sofa in the living room and watched an episode of Law & Order.

"He's the main reason I watch Law & Order, she was referring to Vincent D'Onofrio as Detective Robert Goran." She stated.

"Yeah the way he bends and leans when he's catching them in a fucking lie, it's hilarious". Pete remarked.

They each took a sip of wine, nestled in each other's arms and just chilled.

Norton Kay was moving rapidly on getting programs for needful families who fell subject to crack or any other thing that causes struggles and hard times. He's opened up one of the nation's largest grocery stores. Every pastor in the community invested. Norton got every major pastor in the community to bring the entire tithe and offering money, put it in a Kiddy and broke land for a store that employs 2,000. He was tired of seeing generation after generation of parishioners who give tithe and offering till they die and have nothing for themselves or their children. The pastor and his wife riding around in his and her Bentleys while an eighty year old lady that has been tithing to that same church since she was a child is catching the city bus to church, and having a hard time on making it to the doctor or eat a good meal constantly. They moved on Norton Kay's idea and now the pastors have more profits and the parishioners are blessed with homes, transportation and their children being educated properly. The money and products from the store, circulates through the community like blood through human veins.

Nancy went to the interview and did well. They pulled her background right there at the interview and told her that she could start the next week. She was at an NA meeting when she broke the news of her being hired to Marcy and Teresa. The ladies were sitting in the second row in the huge facility that looked like a ball room.

"So you don't have to go to that hot warehouse anymore, huh." Marcy expressed.

"I'm thanking God as I breathe right now; it's really a beautiful blessing… I owe it all to him." Nancy responded with a radiant beautiful smile.

"I'm glad for you Nancy you deserve it, you're a beautiful spirit, and since you have this less stressful job, all three of us are taking a trip to the UK in a couple of months from now.

Meanwhile Trevor Karp was sent to population. It was an eight room dorm, the cells held three men to each room. Every guy in the cell dorm was engaged in some type of activity whether playing Spades, writing a letter. Some were making a pizza from commissary items pickles, tortilla chips, cheese spreads, and summer sausage. Karp was in his cell room just lying down when a 310pound, 6 foot 5in., blue black, cross eyed brother from Mississippi named Pop Black, who's already completed 30 on a 60 year sentence. He dragged his leg when he walked, it was a cool slow walk which exuded power and confidence. He stood in the doorway of Karp's cell.

"I know you from somewhelse, I just can't picture my mind," Pop said with a crazy ass, deep southern drawl, that will make anybody laugh if they heard it. Karp sat up in his bed. Pop continued.

"You see dem lockers over dare, dem my lockers, all dem my lockers. Dat locker, Dat locker, Dat one over dare, all dats my shit." Karp just looked and kept silent.

"You see all dem boys over dare, dem my boys, Dat one, Dat one, and Dat one". Karp wanted to laugh but held it tight, because he knew the man was sincere, plus Black would kill him and he knew it. Black sucked up the spittle that was oozing from the side of his mouth.

"All dem boys in here... Daze mine, don't fuck wit'em... you hear me nigga."

Karp nodded his head, yes. As Black slowly strode off. Karp was really into staying positive and alive. Prison life had become a tough pill for Trevor to swallow. As he ventured out of his cell into to the area where all the activity was. He walked around each table just trying to familiarize himself with the guys in the cell.

Two young guys came in the dorm, and this guy everyone calls the Professor walked up to one of the young guys and asked.

"What you in for, young brother and how old are you?" The Professor asked.

One of the young men looked around and saw everyone in the cell and spoke quickly.

"Murder...I'm 19!"

Professor blasted.

"Ha Ha, Got damn, Ya'll young niggas out here silly than a mau-fuckah, killing and doing all types of shit... ya'll can't smell pussy up in here, caged up wit a nigga farting all ova ya head and shit. I'm glad I got to be an old man before them motherfuckers hid me. Shiiit I use to be a porno star, I done fucked my share of fine bitches in my lifetime, in the thousands so I'm cool. Oh, I apologize, they call me Professor."

The two young men just looked at Professor and went to their cell. All was cool in the cell and it was Trevor's first day in his new environment. He was still disappointed about not being released. The next morning at breakfast in the cell dorm, each inmate lined up to show his band to the correctional officer to receive his tray. Each man went to a table, six tables to this cell which held twenty-four men. Each placed his tray down and started eating. Pop Black was at the center table and there was no trading or anything at meal time and all of the seasoned inmates knew this. The Professor was the only one who hadn't had an altercation with Pop. The two older gentlemen respected each other. But everyone else in the cell was subject to getting his tray took by the physically dominant, backwater convict Pop Black.

"Yo, I got grits for tha orange juice." Skip Karp shouted across the dorm.

Everyone looked at him, but didn't say anything.

"Damn, I'll make this shit lil better man. I got grits and the eggs for the orange juice."

No one answered, but Pop Black strolled up to him and snatched Karp's entire tray up including the orange juice. All of the prisoners just watched as Skip followed Pop Black back to his table. Black sat down with his tray and Trevor's tray in front of him. Karp stood over him and attempted to grab his tray back. Pop stood up and hit him so hard, that his entire body went sailing lifelessly to the other side of the dorm. Pop Black sat down and everyone went back to eating their breakfast. When the CO's came to get the trays they noticed Karp was lying in the corner in a pool of blood. The officer immediately called his fellow officers and nurses filed in the dorm. Soon followed were the EST's with the gurney that they carried him out on.

"Who did this?" The correctional officer shouted to the entire dorm.

No one answered.

"Alright, all you motherfuckahs are on lockdown."

Most of the guys laughed, and one guy shouted while lying in his cell... "Fuck you, ole corny ass nigga!" Then all went back to their normal activities. Karp was sent to the general hospital where he was diagnosed with blunt trauma to the brain.

FACTS ABOUT CRACK COCAINE

As Sigmund Freud put it The overwhelming Goodness, or pleasure beyond description. Two to Four weeks of Crack Cocaine use leads to addiction, where as heroin or a pain killer like percodan may take months to establish a dependency.

The geek or fiending always follows the use of crack-cocaine, leaving the user in a devastated psychological condition. He or She feels worst off, especially if the individual has no more money or an open avenue to get more crack to smoke. They get desperate, that's when the pawning of items such as furniture, jewelry and cars intercedes, some have went as far as selling their home for little or nothing for another hit of crack. Then there is the robbing and burglary to get more.

The smoker needs a better grade or quality of crack as he goes into father depths of use. The pieces become bigger that he ignites on the stem. As he gets more crack to use, it's basically the same cycle. The euphoric feeling, then as the product diminishes he gets desperate again. Crack use also destroys the small lymphatic vessels that try to clear the body of poisons. Once blocked, these vessels no longer work. Snorting cocaine takes some time to be felt. But if you smoke crack or inject cocaine there is immediate impact- in the smoke, right to the lungs, then to the left side of the heart and to the brain. In the injection, the progress is slightly slower to the right side of the heart, the lungs, the left side of the heart and then the brain.

Freebase or crack-cocaine can be smoked since it vaporizes rather than burns, and because it is fat souble it can readily cross the blood-lung barriers.

For nearly fifteen hundred years the substance has been known to the Peruvian Indians, who have sucked on the coca leaf to relieve their boredom or for ritual observances. As early as 1100's the Incas used cocaine-filled saliva for trephinations—that is, drilling into the skull to relieve pressure on the brain. NOTE: (The powerful central nervous-system stimulant to be a natural alkaloid comes from the Erythroxylon coca).

Then in the 1800,s some twenty years after a German chemist has successfully insulated the pure cocaine from leaves, others began applying the refined alkaloid to various disorders. Freud's experiments with cocaine as an antidepressant led him to try the drug in treatment of various other diseases, among them alcoholisms, morphine addiction and asthma.

Under cocaine therapy for his tuberculosis, Robert Lewis Stevenson wrote The Strange Case of Dr. Jekyll and Mr. Hyde in seventy hours—in 1885. The next year, John Styth Pemberton, an Atlanta druggist, mixed up an elixir of cocaine and caffeine plus some vanilla, fruit and sugar flavoring, then carbonated the potion and called it Coca-Cola.

In 1914, the Harrison Narcotics Act incorrectly labeled cocaine as a narcotic. Something that soothes relieves or dulls sensation. Where as it is instead a powerful stimulant—sharply activating the body. "Almost as if you had stuck your finger in an electric light socket.

Finally, in a 1970, the Comprehensive Drug Abuse Prevention and Control Act classified the substance as a member of Schedule II—high abuse potential with small recognized medical use. In fact, about the only orthodox medical use for more than a century has been to numb the gums for periodontal surgery and to apply local anesthesia to the mucous membranes of the nose, throat and respiratory passages of the upper airway, where a surface—administered local anesthetic is desirable.